The Ophelia Strainge Diaries
Hunks and Hot Pants

Hema Rishi

AuthorHouse™
1663 Liberty Drive
Bloomington, IN 47403
www.authorhouse.com
Phone: 1-800-839-8640

© 2012 by Hema Rishi. All rights reserved.

No part of this book may be reproduced, stored in a retrieval system, or transmitted by any means without the written permission of the author.

Published by AuthorHouse   05/22/2012

ISBN: 978-1-4685-8160-7 (sc)
ISBN: 978-1-4685-8161-4 (e)

Any people depicted in stock imagery provided by Thinkstock are models, and such images are being used for illustrative purposes only.
Certain stock imagery © Thinkstock.

Because of the dynamic nature of the Internet, any web addresses or links contained in this book may have changed since publication and may no longer be valid. The views expressed in this work are solely those of the author and do not necessarily reflect the views of the publisher, and the publisher hereby disclaims any responsibility for them.

Monday 14th February
Bunnies are cute!

Well here we are in deepest darkest February and I'm still in bed. I should be up getting ready but am instead scrawling this on my note pad. It's eight in the morning and life is cruel-I have an hour to get out of my luxuriously fluffy warm pyjamas and into something professional looking. Why? Is the question I ask to the heaven's I most likely won't get an answer as it's far too early for the celestial beings to be awake, getting up simply has to be done despite everything.

The freezing January was a blur of overtime and trying to make up for all the money I spent on unnecessarily expensive presents.

The highlight of my month: Seeing that little grey and pastel pink colour block top that would be perfect with my skinny jeans and gladiator sandals. A fashion statement that is so last season but still relevant because I like the pretty colours! There is something to be said about being eclectic in one's fashion tastes. You can get away with practically anything and put it down to your creative eccentricity. So whatever happens, do not! I repeat do not throw away that neon yellow cropped top from the 1990's.

It has for some miraculous reason managed to stay away from numerous charity collection bags. It is in your wardrobe for a reason; and that's not only because you love it but also because something in the depths of your fashion consciousness has told you to hang on to it.

It is simple fashion karma: What has gone around will come back around again! I'm dreading the return of the shell suit and think going into hiding for a while might be a good idea. Possibly on an island somewhere too hot to wear one of these, so they wouldn't stand a chance!

Still so icy so it has been the best idea to wear my moon boots, these are solely the only way I can walk to work and not fall flat on my face in these adverse weather conditions. If it wasn't for these chunky life savers I would have been stranded indoors for the past month.

No doubt living off scraps of food found in the Singh family kitchen before having to resort to desperate measures. A staple diet of chocolate biscuits and crisps would not have done my rapidly expanding waistline any good.

After these have finished I would then start with the blouses, the soft cotton pastel coloured lovelies before moving onto the shoes but the designer items would have to be left until the end. I would want some time to appreciate them (and how extortionately priced they were) before they are devoured. Before things would get this desperate I hoped that some husky voiced hunk would have found and rescued me.

I'd be air lifted to hospital and treated for cheap clothes-induced malnutrition. Fed on a cocktail drip of Prada and Salvatore Ferragamo for a week to bring my fashion consciousness back to what are considered 'normal' levels. However all of this torture was happily prevented because of the moon boots.

Daydreaming aside venturing outside into the Siberian temperatures and resisting hibernation has not been easy. But I have done it much to the delight of the neighbour's snot nosed pre-adolescents. The group of three or four have on a daily basis strategically placed themselves behind their front gates ready to pelt me with a barrage of rock hard snowballs. These icy bullets resemble cricket balls more than harmless fluffy balls of soft.

I have thus far managed to fend off the little blighters with my thick coat and my stealthy moves. The moonboots have also been an asset when it comes to dodging the ice rocks. But then again anyone would be with thousands of prepared ice stones flying in their direction. There is no way I could have moved like that in heels, even the most microscopic kitten heels would have been lethal. As long as there is a square inch of ice outside Mrs Singh's front door I will not leave the confines of the flat in anything other than the spade soled cosmic numbers.

Strange to think that it's Valentine's Day with most of East London still looking very festive. The fourteenth of February seems to have just crept up on the world like a sneaky child does just before its birthday. It has peered into 'the' cupboard and has been taking a guess as to what is in the parcelled delights. Then 'WHAM'! It's a minute past midnight and the flying chubby cherub child is mauling at the helpless gifts. I feel like one of those defenceless gifts and have done for the past week with my world being mauled at by Valentine's antics. These pink and red bowed beasts are absolutely everywhere! Any amount of available space in every single shop display on the planet has been covered with ribbons and balloons. 'I love you' signs with fluffy teddies holding plush hearts adorn every shelf in retail land. This makes me the Ebenezer Scrooge of Valentine's. Now let's just look at this concept in a little more detail shall we? Everything about the day reminds a person that in order to show their true feelings for the object of their desires they must fork out a considerable sum of money to prove it. This 'proving' of one's love must take the form of a cheap looking tacky stuffed toy or gaudy pink card with sickly sweet message inside. An absolute essential of the day must be the mass produced poetry that any seven year old could surpass in taste and eloquence.

It's not original! Not one bit of it! A hundred other people have exactly the same card! Who would want to wake up on Valentine's Day to a barrage of cards with pink flowers on them, teddy bears and fluffy cute bunnies with cute cotton puff tails with pink ribbons? Ok so they are cute but seriously! Come on if you really loved someone you would buy them jewellery, a flash car or take them away on holiday not calorific chocolates! What would be the point of that when so many of us are on diets so we can fit into that little dress we know our partners love! Give your Valentine something that is useful and no I'm not talking about a new ironing board.

Maybe the reason I am so adamant on how awful Valentine's Day is because nothing has arrived for me in the post . . . Yet! But I remain hopeful that something will, even the smallest of envelops. There must be a myriad of very good obstacles that could have held up the postman. These scenarios range from the absurd like: perhaps he was kidnapped by someone who wanted the hundreds of valentines chocolate there would have been in his bag? To the more rational like maybe he doesn't have moon boots and slipped on the ice? Maybe he was held up with all the deliveries that he has do today. I'm sure he hadn't been yet, he never arrived before 8am, and I always heard the letterbox clink loudly. But just what if he did arrive earlier than expected because of the workload? Maybe Mrs Singh got to my post first? Yes! She could very well be hiding the multitudes of elegantly wrapped parcels and cards that are addressed to me. My blood is positively boiling at the thought of her and Ruby eating the lovely posh chocolates that should be mine! How could this happen? Why didn't I beat them to it? I want my gaudy pink cards with bad poetry and I want them right now!

* * *

Dear reader's you will never will have guessed what has happened to yours truly? The totally unthinkable has occurred. Not to insult your intelligence but never in your wildest imaginings could you ever comprehend what this wonderful thing is! As if the stars had taken their positions in the heavens at exactly the right time for this exquisite twist fate to be carried out! I walked into (more like stomped into) work at about a minute to nine and as immediately confronted with a sour faced Amanda poised with her arms crossed and ready to pounce. If there was ever a day that I didn't need it then this had to be that day! Already annoyed with the post man who still hadn't arrived with what all my Valentines goodies by the time I left for work also every part of me shivered after the ice laced walk to get there. My feet had spread into what could rival Donald Duck's webbed feet in the padded boots and they ached already. This was body modification in its worst sense.
"You are cutting it a bit fine Ophelia!"
I smiled frantically and looked over to the large clock that directly faced the door. There was absolutely no excuse that could be used to get out of this one, but technically there had still been a minute to go! How could a girl explain that she wanted to squeeze out every second that she possibly could waiting by the door for her Valentines cards? Some inner sense

had shouted at me that such an explanation wouldn't go down too well.

". . . Well get yourself sorted ad when you are done come to the office immediately!"

This didn't bode well for the coming day, I left her to put my hand bag and coat in my locker. All the while my mind raced like Usain Bolt with questions like what could I possibly be in trouble for this time?

Amanda was slumped in the chair in front of me, this struck me as odd she was normally very formal. Once again she was in a terrible ensemble so that was some source of comfort.

"There was a parcel that was delivered first thing this morning as I opened up. It was addressed to you, you know we don't allow that sort of thing . . . Well let's just says it's frowned upon!"

And she did frown far too much, one could tell from the very deep lines in her face. Lines that were deepening even more in complete envy by this point! But I wasn't worried about Amanda needing lots of Botox at that point I was far more interested in what this delivery was about! The parcel was for me, it was at last the confirmation I had been waiting for. I knew that in some way that my secret admirer would get in touch. Trying to disguise the quickly widening grin on my face was one of the hardest things I ever had to do. But it was done with great difficulty and through gritted teeth I replied.

" . . . really?"

Note to self: Don't try to do the 'innocent' look, it doesn't work!

"Ophelia I must ask you, did you send the parcel to yourself?"

I instantly mega gasped at the insolence of her question! Even in my desperately single state this thought had never crossed my mind, not once!

"No Amanda, I didn't send anything to myself!"

The corners of her mouth started to twitch unflatteringly and she sniffed indignantly. My eyes worked their way around the shoulder padded colour block jump suit she wore. The forest greens contrasted painfully against the striking parrot pinks and made my eyes sting. Although the morning had not proved to be the best start I had my guiding light. There was something in the building that was waiting for me on Valentine's Day itself! It must have been hand delivered so whoever it was had to be on the premises at some point very early today. It couldn't be anything to do with work or Amanda wouldn't have been so up in arms about it all. This was all so flattering! I Ophelia Strainge was the centre of attention for a good reason for once! I looked up at the lady as we both sat in silence for what seemed like forever; I watched her twitchy lips whimper with rage and what I guessed was just a tiny little bit of jealousy. As terrible as this is to admit I smiled inside knowing that this was driving her mad.

"So can I see my parcel?"

The boss sniffed once again before nodding at the office door.

"The girls have it outside!"

I stomped my way out into the main arena that was the public library and demanded my prize.

"Where is it then?"

My maniacal gaze flew over every work surface looking for a parcel that would vaguely resemble a Valentine. As if my eyes were pre-programmed to instantly detect anything pink, red or resembling cheap velvet I scanned over surfaces for heart or teddy bear shaped objects but to no avail.

Lucy smiled at my desperation as she watched my flailing frustration. In hindsight I should have played it cool and made out that it wasn't that much of a big deal, but it was! It so really was!

The Flashback: The last time I received a Valentines was when I was thirteen years old, the age every little girl craves some acceptance from the opposite sex. A cheap and tacky valentine's card symbolises that she is doing something right.

It said that if she was to continue doing what she was doing she would one day grow up to be an equally successful and attractive female. But that wondrous day for me wasn't what it should have been. The clinking of the metal letter box had at first signified the ultimate dream! I remember running to the front door like a bloodthirsty wolf, every limb worked in over drive to get me there before anyone else. Like a true Olympian I reached my destination out of breath and ready to pass out with extreme exhaustion, but I was prepared to suffer that for the prize that lay in wait. I was willing to do anything for this acceptance.

If memory serves me correctly the pristine cream coloured card had been hand delivered to the door; my grubby teenage paws grabbed it and my widened eyes looked lovingly all over the silver script on the front. 'Ophelia' was written in beautiful handwriting, the silver ink flashed across the surface with every movement. At that point there was nothing else more beautiful in existence.

My chunky fingers tore through the envelope ripping the cover to get to my dreams.

"Any post for me?"

My father chimed from the living room, there was a slight squeak at the end of his voice and he knew . . . He always knew! But I didn't care and continued with my excavating.

"No post for you!"

I screeched back and a fleeting thought flew through my mind. Did my parents ever give each other Valentine's Day cards? This was a scary thought to a thirteen year old who didn't want to imagine her parents being all romantic. How hideous would that be? It didn't bear thinking about! No! My mind quickly flipped back to the task in hand. I pulled out the glistening card from its sleeve. The card was handmade quite obviously, looking back a bit gaudy but I wasn't complaining! On the front a crude bunny rabbit drawn in what looked like thick crayon. It held a red splodge. This had to be a heart or a squashed tomato.

But seeing as it had been the fourteenth of February I guessed it was a heart. But finally the real thing had come my way and that's all that mattered. But who was it from? Could it have been Ben? My thirteen year old self was totally in love with him! The most amazing boy in my class! Ben was brilliant at absolutely everything he did, even maths and science. In fact I remembered enjoying science a lot more because of his mere presence. I loved his strawberry blonde hair and the way he tilted his head to the side when he was thinking. He was by far the tallest boy in the class, almost as tall as the form tutor. I thanked the stars daily that they had seen it fit for me to be in the same form group as him; life just wouldn't have been the same without Ben!

Flipping open the card clumsily I hoped he had seen the light and known that I was the only one for him, that we should be married one day when we were grown-ups and spawn lots of beautiful children.

"Dear Ophelia, Happy Valentine's Day,

Just because I know what it's like to not get one either! Love Rachael"

My whole world could have smashed into pieces! It wasn't from the lovely Ben but my friend Rachael. Although what she did was very thoughtful it was at the same time devastating and left me hating the 14th of February with a total passion. Until now that is! Now many years later here I am with this time what I hope is a real Valentine's and not another well-meant hoax.

"Where is it then?"

My eyes flailed around like a total lunatic!

"Where's what?"

Lucy had always hated me and at that moment I knew it for sure, she was enjoying playing mind games with me! It was incredibly mean to make me wait longer than necessary to receive my Valentines. We were in a stand-off she was ready, every limb in her body waiting for me to pounce. I could see that she guarded the counter shelf with her body, it had to be there!

Lucy at that moment realised that she was in danger of revealing her true possessive and competitive tendencies. I could see it on her eyes as they flitted from side to side whenever she was about to back down. She knew that this wouldn't go down well she had to be seen to be normal, even borderline rational if she was to get that chance for promotion. Smoothing down her dress she flashed me her welcoming public smile, it was as fake as they come. Each one of her perfectly straight whitened teeth were on show in that slightly demonic grin of hers.

She shrugged for a moment before reaching down below the counter (as suspected!) and pulled out the prized possession. Wasting no time I needed to know what all this was about. The envelope was baby pink, nothing abnormal there so far. Then a surge of déjà vu overcame me as I once again ripped open the envelope semi cautiously semi ecstatically. Could this be a repeat of what had happened to me all those years ago? Would I be totally devastated if it was from a friend instead of that totally hot guy in the Café across the road?

This time the card had a puppy dog on the cover and it sat happily in a tea cup. This was the cutest thing I had ever seen. It was fluffy overload as I peeled back the front cover in expectant ecstasy at what was to come. Wanting this moment to be prolonged forever I watched the faces of my extremely jealous colleagues as they stood still waiting for me to open the card.

" . . . Whose it from then?"

Milla our work experience girl piped in.

" . . . You're not supposed to know that's the whole point!"

Lucy was tres annoying whenever the opportunity arose, it was just her way.

But I wanted to know so I flipped open the glossy card, the simple message read:

"From your biggest fan . . . X"

How did this person know that my most absolute favourite film of all time was Stephen King's Misery? This did frighten me a tad but only for a moment as I lovingly stroked the surface of my very first real Valentine's card. I could have shed a tear at the years I had spent waiting for this very moment, but it had been worth the wait. I had finally been elevated to the upper echelons of desirables.

"Well?"

I shrugged honestly and flicked my hair back past my neck in the way that the popular girls do.

"I don't know"

One was very close to adding something like 'I don't know and am not really bothered as I have a hundred parcels like these at home to unwrap later on!' but I held myself back.

" . . . What's in the parcel then?"

This was like a double dose of joy, a parcel as well! Fate was well and truly making up for all those lonely disappointed Valentines days over the years.

Again I tore through the pink floral wrapping paper that matched the envelope, whoever this was had really made the effort to make this special—Could it truly have been a man? The mind really did boggle.

Peeling off the last remnants of paper revealed a very fluffy teddy bear and a bag of heart shaped Haribo gummy sweets.

My audience watched on in silence as I revelled in that lovely Valentine's glow. The best feeling since I bagged that Velveteen dress in the sales for half the price beating off my competitor by inches! My hand had reached the sale rail a split second before hers did. The feeling of Victory was beyond even beyond it truly was awesome. So as you can imagine the rest of my day was spent walking on air, I didn't know who it was from and I didn't care—The main thing was that I had received an actual real live Valentine's card for the first time ever (even though I haven't found out who it is from, and probably never will) I am now St Valentine's biggest official fan of all time! Bring on the sickly pink and red bows I want them everywhere!

Friday 4th March
Wooden Wedges

Amanda decided last week to send me on the yearly customer services training course in Central London. I had been on the day's course the same time last year; I don't remember much of it apart from the lovely sandwiches they provided at lunchtime. If memory serves me correctly I had a three cheese double decker type culinary concoction (it was as it said on the packet made up of three different types of cheeses). Needless to say I loved how it hit the spot, not sure it did my blood pressure any good though. The amount of cheese in this thing must have struck fear into the very core of every artery in my body for a long time after that day.

They got over it in time and seem to be happy enough now; I know this from the last health check-up. But one has decided to go easy on them from then on no matter how delicious the lunchtime lovelies on offer prove to be. Today as mentioned above is a Friday. This is the greatest day of the week as it signals tomorrow being freedom for two days. Normally this would have been great but today I had to spend it in the most congested city in the world! I loathed getting up and having to face the inevitable train delays.

Mornings like this were the catalyst for wanting another job, one where I could have a lay in of a morning. Or even better not have to go into work on Fridays at all.

A career as a superstar fashion blogger would not go a miss; I could get up whenever I wanted to a barrage of calls from high end fashion magazines desperately needing my work. Desperation meant that I would even consider pet sitting or child minding (same thing different job titles in my opinion). Anything to get away from the madness of a regular nine to five, alas one had rent to pay. I looked at all the miserable grey faces on the tube that wanted exactly what I had wanted—to be back in bed snuggled up under the duvet. If only life was that simple! I let out a giant sigh at my thoughts, this was greeted by an annoyed look from the teenage boy sitting opposite me. I scoffed inside at his insolence and total lack of fashion sense. Wait until he had to get a job, his future employers would strongly insist on him pulling his trousers up! He would have to pull them so high that they actually stayed around his waist and not half way down his thighs. Some fashion trends were a mystery even to me, I really wasn't down with the kids and was quite happy about that.

'It's always good to brush up on your interpersonal skills!'

No kidding boss! What I wasn't able to get my head around was why I seemed to be the popular choice to go? Lucy wasn't interested at all and apparently hid in the office until the decision had been made. I was practically pushed to the front of the queue; perhaps I was seen to have been over keen?

The whole picking and choosing process was bewildering but it meant one less day of being in the same building as gossiping Amanda and Lucy and that was a perk in itself.

On the plus side, and there was a very big plus side in this case: One also got to pass my most favourite department store of all time. This didn't happen very often so I jumped at the chance. One of the most beautiful shopping experiences in London, it could rival any new out of town shopping complex. Everybody loves Selfridges, with its beautiful chrome structure and gorgeous Art Deco exterior. Butterflies took over me whenever I stepped through the decadent store entrance; each time meant walking into a new more glamorous world.

However real magic happened to me that morning when I walked in through the heavy ornate doors and onto the crisp clean marble floor of the store. My head was in a spin as slowly my surroundings made themselves clear to me. My eyes hurt as they adjusted to the absolute beauty of everything! I loved it and wanted more of this retail wonderland as my eyes darted around from item to beautiful new shiny item. Each handbag, pair of shoes and other object was placed strategically on individual plinths that stood like mini monoliths around me. Each had been positioned like a trail of breadcrumbs that I was helpless to resist. My heart pounded harder with each step into the store and it wouldn't be long until I would faint in total desire. I soon peaked as my wandering eyes became set on something that had totally taken my breath away.

An item of such beauty and grace that I really knew that fainting was not far off. I looked frantically for a place to sit before my legs gave way in this fashion ecstasy, there were low cushioned seats and went for them fast. Once sitting down I took time to take in the object of my affections. A glorious pair of United Nude Geisha Style wedges. The heels on the shoes could have been skyscrapers, they were absolutely huge. Window cleaners could don a pair of these and no longer need ladders!

These pieces of fashion art were a serious health and safety hazards anyone who could manage to put their feet in them and attempt to walk—But I totally loved them. Even with the major risk of head banging on even the highest of ceilings. With

a chunky heel to die for I could in effect be just as tall as the giant supermodel assistant who was by then waiting on me.
"Can I help you?"
Her bright perfectly mascaraed eyes were fixed on my sad and floppy form on the seat. Her crisp French accent was to die for; there was something so pristine and stern about it. I looked up at her it was obvious more than help was needed here, something of a more liquid nature and stronger. But assistance with the shoes would be a good start. The shop assistant looked as though she was bred specifically for this purpose. Possibly in human sized pods on a special island some obscure and 'undiscovered by tourists' corner of the Indian Ocean. Hundreds of these immaculate store assistants are harvested and only emerging from their pods once ready. They come complete with tailored skirt suits, flawless skin and perfect pouts ready to take on the great public. The one that had spotted me and had come my way was no different. Tall and slender the lady wore eye-wateringly high heels which complimented her hollow cheeks and beautiful pout.
Hard to think of a pout being gorgeous but hers was. Her body language translated as something like 'If it's the last thing I ever do I'm going to make you wear those shoes and you are going to love them and buy them! I am going to show you and your credit card no mercy!'
It was all so totally fabulous! I loved being hunted down as bizarre as that may sound (don't judge me on that last sentence!)
She arrived by my side with precision timing.
"Erm yes, I'd like to take a closer look at those"
In my most professional sounding voice, I thought it was fairly good despite the excited trembling that was uncontrollable. My weak and feeble voice managed to somehow stammer at her eager-to-please expression. Her knowing smile stretched across her jaw but miraculously there were no signs of crow's feet at the corners of her eyes. Was this the doing of Botox or the fact that she is an immortal and therefore is immune to any signs of aging?
"I'm a size 4.5"

"Let me see if I can find a pair for you"
She nodded and trotted off in her heels to what I guessed was an amazing treasure trove of a stock room. Waiting like one would do in a doctor's surgery it was painful but it would be worth it once my hands were on the prize! The realisation hit me while I was waiting for the return of the glamorous assistant with my shoes. Would these shoes be road-worthy? Yes sure they were gorgeous and lovely to look at but would I be able to actually walk in them? Secondly and a little more importantly would I be able to afford them? Did I not realise that there is in fact a recession going on? These thoughts panicked me. Taking a deep breath helped steady my thoughts a little, I made myself as comfortable as possible without looking as though a 'freak out' was on the cards.

"Hold it together girl!"
I muttered under my breath while my heart raced excitedly around my chest. Before I felt the full onslaught of another 'pass out' moment the assistant returned. I had without realising already taken off my current worn out flats, with tootsies out and ready for action. I thanked my stars that I had a pedicure only a week ago, things could have gotten ugly. She skipped the part where she would normally ask me to 'take a seat and make myself comfortable' I had done this too many times before-I knew the drill, it was now just about waiting for the grand opening of the box.

She knelt down on the floor beside me and for that moment I was a princess! So far so good—or maybe she was preparing me for the epic fail that would be walking in them? But it had felt nice so far so I went along with it.

Dramatically she pulled open the lid to reveal yet another layer of packaging! Sheesh, these really seemed to be a coy pair of shoes! It's wouldn't matter I would soon make them feel at home like I had done with others so many times before. Her well-manicured fingernails continued to work peeling back the many layers of paper that surrounded my prize. (My apologies if my descriptions resemble those of a really bad porno, I have to work on my descriptive narrative but rest assured I am)

At last we got there and she took the shoes out of the box and time itself could have stopped! There they were bright bold and definitely beautiful, holding my breath I placed one foot inside one shoe. The feeling of absolute bliss surrounded me as mine were the first feet to feel the pristine perfectness of the fabric upper of the shoe. Then once again the second one closely followed by the same feeling of total ecstasy. A second later and one was ready to move in them. With the help of the unconvinced shop assistant the muscles in my calves prompted me upwards. I stood and to my absolute joy and found that I was able to look over the heads of absolutely everyone who had been on the ground floor.

This really was pure magic life couldn't get better than this, the giant wedges must have put at least seven inches of height onto my short munchkin-like fame.

There was however one slight problem . . .

Being upright and staring over everyone was great fun but it wasn't going to help me get around. One need to walk and I couldn't! The only way I could ever wear these beauties would be if I stood completely still, this was a truly terrifying thought.

"Here hold my arm and try!"

The assistant was more determined than I was at getting me mobile. Her hopeful tone and gaze spurred me on; I had never been as intimate with a pod grown darling as I was then. A strange sensation but she was someone who would grow on me. A better salary would enable me to have of my very own assistants! She would cater to my every shopping whim making me the envy of every fashionista in town! Alas that wasn't going to happen just yet but it was something to aim for when I did finally strike it lucky.

So there I was in the middle of the floor and bandy legged, my ankles together but my knees as far apart as was physically possible. My pelvis pushed forwards in attempt to try and even out the balance of the pose—No not a good idea! But determined I piped up and asked in a pathetically whispery way that inevitably eternal question that every shopper at some point will ask:

"How much are they?"
The assistant smiled now the creases appeared as if from nowhere at the corners of her eyes. They deepened intensely, was she melting or was this what happened when she got down to business?
"They are one hundred and ninety eight pounds"
That's two hundred pounds from my meagre monthly wage.
"Oh right"
That's two hundred pounds that really should be going on my rent.
"Ah so can I . . ."
That's two hundred pounds that should be put in a savings account so that one day I may be able to afford important things like a house and a car, things that regular people have!
The same knowing smile appeared once again.
"Yes of course you can think about it!"
Neatly packing the extortionately priced beauties back in to their box, I could have cried out in total anguish.
"But wait! Hold on . . . !"
The assistants eyes lit up starkly contrasting against her pale Number 09 Ivory foundation covered face. The inner turmoil that was happening was indescribable now that they had been put back in the box. I had a chance to really consider the pros and cons, sexy personified these shoes had the power to wow and surprise with every step that the wearer took in them (any that they were able to that is). There was the fact that on first entering the department store every cell that made up my being was magnetised just at the mere sight of them—they had practically called me over to them! I could learn to walk in them surely, if I practiced for half an hour each day I would get the hang of it by summer! I would be able to walk around the bedroom to begin with and then maybe soon think about tackling the staircase. It could be done if I was dedicated enough and I was! Yes I Ophelia who has banded about in the narrowest of stilettoes before would most definitely be able to make it in these wooden wedges!
I needed saving from myself more than ever that day, or should I say my wallet needed saving from me as I flipped it out and

before one could say 'obsession with recession' I had done the unthinkable.
"Do you Accept Visa?"
The words flew from my lips as easily as breath did.
"Yes we do I will pack them up for you"
Falling into a slump on the plush seating, I was too exhausted by this experience to think. But I had to think more than ever. The fear of God shot through me as a chance glance up at the clock on the marbled wall made me shudder in fear. It read a quarter past nine, this wasn't good as I had to be at the 'Customer Services' training course fifteen minutes ago! A very annoyed Amanda would no doubt be calling at moment screeching and demanding to know why I wasn't there. She wouldn't let this one go, she never did. But I was not leaving without the shoes after coming this far with them. The next few minutes were a blur mingled in with most of Oxford Street flashing past me like the rest of the day had.

* * *

"Hai! You spent two hundred pounds on Chappals!"
"It's not that bad Mum! People spend a lot more on shoes these days! It's not 1965 anymore you know"
Ruby very nearly got a slap to the back of her head; her mother wasn't impressed at the cheekiness.
Ruby and Mrs Singh debated my purchase at the kitchen table. It was slightly worrying that both Mrs Singh's hands were on her head in a sort of 'Oh my God' position. What was nice was that her 'ever stroppy' teenage daughter Ruby was for once actually sticking up for me.
"People spend thousands on shoes these days; you have to pay for quality!"
Hands on hips she managed to dodge the last potential smack and was ready for the next one her mother would no doubt attempt. She didn't care and looked the total epitome of acne scarred adolescent cool.
"Let's see them then!"

Her wide eyes yearned for me to open up the box and show her the goodies, I obliged as a reward for her acceptance.
One of the Geisha style shoes was pulled out to gasps from my captivated audience, the ladies sat and watched in total silence for a moment before:
"Haaaaaaa!"
Mrs Singh clutched her chest as if a heart attack wasn't far away, while Ruby stood in awe struck shock. It was hard to gauge what the general consensus was so I waited hoping for some sort of approval. Seconds later it came.
"Oh my goodness you're gonna look like a total babe in those, that's going to make you look really tall!"
Mrs Singh went and sat down; she mopped her brow with her apron as she did this.
"Where are you going to wear these things then?"
Her flat palm pointed at the box accusingly.
" . . . What made you buy them?"
The shoes looked monumental within the confines of the flat, there definitely wasn't the same effect there had been in the deceptively spacious department store.
"Are they the right size?"
"Yeah what size are they? Can I borrow them?"
Erm no Ruby, no you can't! My brain screamed this out to her. I by then felt like a total fool, but a fool with something to prove. My wearing them out would prove to Mrs Singh that I would look amazing in them regardless of what she thought. It simply had to be done! Rebel with a cause it is possible to be a diva, wear things that are not considered 'normal' and look fabulous in them. This would involve walking in them and obviously would take some time, but with a little determination one could do this.
"I love them! I so think you should keep them Oppy!"
I hated it when I got called that but nevertheless appreciated the support.
"Thanks I will Rubes!"
She shot me that look of teenage defiance and thankfully got the point instantly; while Mrs Singh was completely oblivious to the friendly tension between me and her daughter. She

pushed herself out of the chair she was slumped in and shook her head as she left to get on with cooking the family meal. Ruby and I were left gazing longingly at the pair of wedges, both head over heels in love with them! It felt good to know that someone else could appreciate the same beauty and understand the feelings that one felt when simply observing them. She felt the same jolt of electricity as I did. I looked over at Ruby still in her school uniform of navy blue sweat shirt with trousers and looking very scruffy. But there was hope for her yet; she obviously had a keen eye for fashion which for someone her age was a fantastic start in life—well I thought so anyway.

I am wearing them now as I write this entry. Cross legged on the chair at my desk I ponder on the fact that many women and some men teach themselves how to walk in heels. I have done this myself and often prance about on stilettoes. There was absolutely no reason why I couldn't do the same with these wedges. For those who practically live in heels these Geisha wedges would pose absolutely no threat at all. Ok first step is to stand in them again . . . Watch this space!

Saturday 23rd April
Pre Wedding jitters!

Don't worry it's not me! I wouldn't go and do something silly like that! But there is no way I can avoid mentioning 'The Wedding'. Yes royalty's golden couple are finally getting hitched after years of speculation. The whole world knows about it and is bracing itself for the big day with gusto including Mrs Singh, rather reluctantly her husband Mr Singh and Ruby. All of this is a fairly odd experience even more so in the case of Ruby's enthusiasm for the whole event. It normally took something virtually impossible and usually a little morbid to rouse the teenager's interest. She like everyone else seemed to be lapping it up.

Underneath the cool but moody exterior were clearly the outlines of a potential grown up. This was a good sign and I was genuinely happy at the thought that she may join us in the ranks of humankind. Back to this morning's proceedings and I left my bedroom thinking I was in a different house. The science fiction-like feeling was strong in a Star Wars way; could this be what alien abduction was like? The bannisters had been decked in the faithful blue, red and white. The entrance to the house along with most of the living room has been decked out with bunting and photographs of the happy couple.

"Do you like them? I got them off the net!"

They were everywhere; the living room was practically wallpapered with them.

"Yes my Ruby is so clever!"

Her mother pinched her cheek with as much force as she could muster. This looked rather painful and I felt for the girl.

"Ouch Mum that really hurts!"

"Sorry darling!"

In fact most of the street seemed to be decked out in the Union Jack for the twenty-ninth of April.

Despite it being an extremely happy occasion one can't help but wanting to hide. I am totally overwhelmed by the real need to go and camp out on a deserted island for a week or so, or at least until it all dies down—If it ever does!

Setting up a stall on the beach that sold jewellery made from sea shells and pretty pebbles would be the way I would make ends meet. Yes I am an old stick in the mud! I really should be in the same orb of expectant awe that the rest of the country is in. To some extent I am a little curious about it, for example I too desperately have to see 'the wedding dress' and the gorgeous smile that will be inevitable on the blushing bride. Perhaps I'm just insanely jealous? Am I simply annoyed that I have not bagged myself an eligible bachelor yet despite there being one or two hopefuls?

There is a strong possibility that this is the case as it has been with all those lone and barren Valentine's Days.

If this is the case then I scold myself now for being a spoil sport and will join everyone else in congratulating the young couple. I'm sure my mother is also enjoying the festivities from the family home in South Woodford. One can just see her now watching the Royal wedding on the twenty-ninth wringing her wrists in total frustration. She would angrily mutter under her breath something about not being invited. She thought my ex-boyfriend was royalty, as did I when we first met but that's always the way in the beginning of all relationships for me. Thing's tend to turn sour pretty quickly after the initial adoration wears off. This worrying pattern was one that I have on numerous occasions vowed to break out of, that was until the next handsomely regal face comes along.

But marriage itself is a strange concept.

My views of it have always been that it had to be something like what my parents had been in for a million years. An 'arrangement' where my mother would constantly snap about something or another and my father would simply grunt quietly. He'd look up for a second and then straight back down at the paper he would be hiding behind. Is that what eventually happened to those couples who were in love at some point in their youth? The Singh's were exactly the same, only difference was that Mrs Singh screeched at her husband in Punjabi. I guess it was about the same sort of mundane thing.

The royal couple look like they are head over heels and amazingly in love. Like my parents obviously had to be at some point in the 1800's when they actually liked one another! Enough to get married at least anyway, so just what is their secret to a long and happy marriage? This is a question that is far too involved to even comprehend right now. That one is to be kept bubbling on the back burner for a while and pondered on at a later date.

In the meantime I'm dragged out of my daydream by royal wedding merchandise that is everywhere! I switch on the clapped out old TV set in my room and it's on every one of the freeview channels. There's no escaping it! Everything from the usual egg cups and tea cosies to royal wedding condoms. Union jack covered thimbles and matching t-shirts have been on all the market stalls in existence since the wedding date was set.

There is a light to the end of this tunnel-and that's the 'Mistake' Souvenir mug with the future brother-in-laws name instead of the grooms. How awkward is that? You can't help but think that perhaps someone somewhere in a souvenir mug making factory thought that this would be a great idea!

These 'wrong' gaudy looking mugs are now very sought after online, eBay is auctioning them for a minimum of £100. I am half tempted (possibly a little bit more like three quarters tempted) to bid on one of these myself, the only thing stopping me from putting in my maximum bid of £1000 is whether I can afford to part with the money for a piece of history. Could this be the sort of thing that would just grow in value with the years? Would I be a total millionaire in five years' time? Anglophiles from all corners of the globe will be approaching me in their droves begging me to let them have it. I will have to give this a lot of serious intense thought as it could well be the investment of a lifetime! Or perhaps the very fact that you are reading this indicates that I have far too much time on my hands.

* * *

Now nearly two in the morning and I'm still recovering from the traumatic experience of an hour ago. It was at about half past midnight when 'it' happened. All the family had gone to sleep and I tip toed down the stairs into the kitchen where the computer is. Luckily they had upgraded to a new PC so it's now very swish and fancy—luckily for me it didn't make very much noise when getting started like its predecessor had done. That old thing could have been connected to a larger hamster wheel that the Singh's cat Missy could have run in. She would have generated her own source of electricity for the machine it being one of the most unreliable things ever known to mankind.
Straight onto the auction site, I was there in moments.
The lowest bid for any of the five mugs was £124.95 with still a whole week to go. The choice to walk away from all was there; to spend the rest of the evening forgetting about frivolous ways to spend my hard earned cash would have made sense. On the other hand I could get hold of one of these gross

ceramic mistake's and with a bit of careful looking after (I'm thinking a thick walled ultra-secured safety deposit box in a very reputable bank for several years) this would most likely be one of the most financially savvy moves ever made.

That was at the point at which it stopped being a matter of making the decision—there was no turning back and getting back to bed. Going for it was the only real option left, crystal clear by then in my mind that this would be the right sort of investment for the future.

Sixteen bidders were also vying for the same prize, I competing against serious art collectors here no doubt. People who would have a lot more funding than me, but I flat out refused to give in and let doubt get the better of me. Just what if I got it? This 'desperate wanting' of old bits of toot was what must have kept auction houses in business for years.

Before I knew it the desire overwhelmed me as I glazed over the ceramic work of art. I typed in my bid; my fingers had a mind of their own and just let rip. £300.00 on the first cup that came up, surely this was reasonable enough a price for such a thing? Adrenaline pumped and heartbeat pounded through my body furiously. Dizzying and exciting at the same time, this was as high octane as one could get in ones pyjamas.

I waited with baited breath hoping that my bid was high enough that it would guarantee getting hold of the mug. It had to be! Who in their right mind would pay that much for something that was a fluke? I was safe in the knowledge that it was mine for a few seconds, after which a message flashed across my screen.

'You have been outbid! Please enter a higher bid now'

An insane furiousness took hold of me! How could this be? Before thinking shaking with an inconsolable anger the next bid went in.

'£450.00', then the 'Enter' keyboard key was pressed with pride.

Ha! Now who was winning? Me that's who! Stick that in your pipe mister or missus eBay bidder!

"You have been outbid! Please enter a higher bid now"

Not being able to believe my misfortune I actually stopped to think for a moment. They would probably top the highest bid so just to annoy them I was going to do the unthinkable. I mopped my by then sweating brow with the sleeve of my cotton pyjama top and took a deep breath.

'£650.00' with a short moment's pause between typing that in and pressing the 'Enter' key, over two thirds of my wage could have potentially been squandered over a ceramic thing. Mrs Singh would surely kick me out for a month if the rent wasn't on time again; she was getting fed up of the constant excuses I had come up with.

"You have been outbid! Please enter a higher bid now"

Ok this was the absolutely the last bid . . .

'£950.00'

What was I doing? This really was insane! There on the screen was my whole month's wages in black and white.

Was this a mistake? YES! I was by this point seriously praying that the eBayer who was competing would outbid me.

"Come on, come on, come on!"

The seconds ticked away on the online clock in the corner of the screen.

Then it happened

"You have been outbid! Please enter a higher amount"

Never happier to see those words in my life I could have cried! They could have the blasted thing I didn't want it! Being a financially responsible grown up was a much better feeling. After all our monthly income needs to be used on rent and other bills and not on shoes or things like really expensive cups!

The computer was turned off in a flash as I dashed up stairs to practically make love to my credit card. I love that plastic card!

Friday 29th April
The Big Day!

To say today had been one of the most momentous days of my life would be a gross understatement. It began like this: An early start on the wedding day wasn't planned as I had been looking forwards to a lazy day. One filled with flicking channels on the television, eating spicy corn crisps from the one pound shop (excellent value and helps cut the costs of my junk food addiction) a relaxed morning is what I felt I deserved. After all it wasn't every day that we had a royal wedding! I intended to make the most of it.

Trotting downstairs I made my way to the kitchen to see what could be rustled up for breakfast. Something very high in fat and greasy would be a fantastic start to my lazy and unhealthy day. I was immediately confronted with a scene that was as far from normal as was possible. The whole family had obviously been up for hours preparing because the kitchen smelt delicious! Mrs Singh was packing what looked like a picnic basket. From the scent in the kitchen I wanted desperately to be able to dive into it.

Even Ruby had combed back that floppy fringe to look vaguely presentable—there was still a little more work to do but she was almost there. What frightened me the most about the scene was Mr Singh; he was a normally quiet man, serious but relaxed a lot of the time. He was usually always turned out smartly no matter what time of the day. This morning was no different however there was something else odd about him.

I had never seen him do this 'odd' thing before, he was actually smiling! Yes the man had a set of straight white and perfect teeth—all together quite a dazzling smile. Dare I say it but I saw straight away how he would have been quite a catch in his younger years! Beyond the grey hair he was . . . No! I must stop this is not a good track to go down. Back to my story but I could have fainted in shock.

"We are going to see the wedding!"

Mrs Singh buzzed with pride but was she crazy? Did she not know that even if she had managed to actually get anywhere near the action she and the rest of the family would be squashed. Tins of Sardines! Only they would be human sardines if nothing else—surely the best way to see the wedding would have been at home on the television? But as I thought about it a little more I realised that deep down inside, underneath the apron and past the rolling pin there was a woman who was up for a party. Well apart from when she wore the sour expression at my rolling into the flat at two in the morning on numerous occasions. Sitting down at the kitchen table I watched Ruby practice her curtsies, Mrs Singh continue to prepare a picnic and Mr Singh excitedly read through the wedding edition papers. The buzzing activity that was happening all around me was infectious—I liked it.

"Come with us Ophelia!"

Ruby discarded her moody teenage attitude and had obviously had far too much caffeine already. The girl was positively shaking with excitement. Even if you had wanted to hide away from the mass hysteria as I had done until then the chances were that somewhere deep down inside you did want to at least see a real princess. By this point I really was starting to get sucked into the fervour Yes I was going to do it and go with them! Never mind that we probably wouldn't see anything but it was the fact that we were going to be a part of history albeit in a very miniscule way!

"Yes Ok if you wouldn't mind terribly . . . I will then!"

I pulled on my glitziest top and jazziest pair of skinny jeans with peep toe kitten heels. The kitten heels were a purple/cerise colour and had matching gold and purple sequins all over them. These were disco shoes that would have made Olivia Newton-John proud. The heels were a little bit higher than 'kitten' but today this was forgivable as I would need as much height as possible. No doubt there would be grannies clinging onto the lampposts and railings outside Buckingham Palace. This caused for something more than just forwards planning, one simply had to be mega prepared for the day. What about a cardigan? No as this would cover up the glitzy gold top that I would want everyone to see.

Hopefully just hopefully a rouge BBC camera would pick me up, a wave to my mother while swinging from a lamp post was the genius plan. She would no doubt be watching and taking note of everything she saw. Seeing me making a fool of myself on national television would drive her insane, this in turn would make the day even sweeter. You must understand that ours really is a love hate relationship. The family car was a trusty old maroon hued Volvo that didn't get to see the light of day

very much. It was a tight fit with all of us, the top of Mr Singh's turban just skimmed the roof of the car as he expertly body popped his large frame into the driving seat. He revved the engine the keys jingled with all the key chains that hung from it; the car sounded as if it had a very bad chest infection and then decided to switch itself off.
"Come on come on Jaldi Chalooo!"
He wasn't going to give up and his chunky hands turned the key again. The intense silent look that had taken over his face showed that he meant business. Mr Singh was not someone to be messed about with, especially not when it came to getting the car started. With a jerk of the keys in the ignition he almost willed the car to work. It sputtered again before giving up for the second time.
"Maybe we should just stay home and watch it on the tele!"
Ruby huffed. She was in the back with me and the several bags along with the basket of food packed. We had both somehow negotiated a comfortable position seeing as we were going to be in the back of the Volvo for a while.
"No Ruby! We are going!"
"Yes just be quiet your Dad is sorting it!"
She huffed once again as her father grumbled something under his breath and then angrily once again turned the key planted in the ignition; he used all the strength he could muster with an almighty growl. Mr Singh's braun worked and the car started up.
"So are you still going out with that guy then? What's his name? He hasn't come round for ages!"
Ruby had a school girl crush on Neville, after all what young girl wouldn't? He was rich he was handsome, even laughed at my jokes in-between business calls; he was perfect in every way possible. But she was right I hadn't heard from him in a long time. Trying to keep my mind off this fact was difficult and I so wished that she hadn't brought it up.
" . . . Ruby! Shut up!"
If her father didn't have two hands on the steering wheel it would have been a quick slap to the back of her head. Her comments had got me thinking about things: how much time

would need to lapse between the end of the last phone call or text and the present before a relationship was officially deemed 'over'? This was definite day time TV material. Neville seemed to have disappeared from the face of the earth!

I had left numerous phone calls and text messages but again how long could one continue to try and contact someone before ones behaviour went into 'stalking' territory? Police knocking at the door with a warning would not be desirable, even worse if it ever got around at work. Amanda would absolutely delight in this I could picture her sour old face with more than a hint of glee. Sebastian the village loudspeaker would make it known throughout the land while Lucy would just languish in news of my epic fail.

"I'm really sorry Ophelia but we have to let you go, we can't really have a stalker working for us!"

I would be handed my P45 and a big wave.

Another thought I had while resisting the temptation to have a very quiet rummage around in the dream picnic basket was that perhaps somehow Neville found out about Cole? But how could he know of the New Year's night I spent with my head on the kitchen table? If he knew that then he would have surely also known that nothing happened between us. My mind whirred and what I needed was one of the posh custard creams that I distinctively saw Mrs Singh pack in the basket that morning.

Before the picnic sneak however I needed to survey my surroundings, to make sure no one would notice my nimble fat fingers prise their way in through the lid. Ruby next to me by then was plugged into her iPod, the value pack of burger baps on top of the basket vibrated to the thumping bass. Mr Singh quite obviously was fully concentrating on the road ahead, his mission to dodge the traffic. He muttered to himself something about the best route into inner London, today however there was no such thing.

But Mrs Singh! Well she was on the ball as ever, nothing got past her. There was a psychic connection with me I could see her dark eyes surveying my form expectantly in the rear view mirror. There was no way even with my most stealthy moves that I could grab just one small rectangular delight. The corners of her mouth did that downward turning thing that happened whenever she disagreed with anything. There was nothing for it but to starve until she, the queen and ruler of all picnic baskets would deem the time and place suitable to indulge in its culinary contents.

Judging from the glorious scents in the kitchen this morning it was to be worth the wait.

The car ride into London was fraught with hurdles as one would expect on a day like this. Crazy people dressed as members of the royal family seemed to be everywhere. While this would have normally been hilarious it was exceedingly annoying. Crazy people who had obviously started out early on the booze along with my by then hurting feet made me more susceptible to being aggravated. They had hardly been worn regardless of being in my wardrobe for possibly a year! This had been a bad time to realise this. Too late now unless I wanted to pad around the city bare footed, no thank you not with all those pieces of chewed up gum splodges and pigeon droppings that I would undoubtedly step on. I would keep my twinkled shoes on and would hope to get through today without too much trouble. Looking good was sometimes painful and my sore toes really highlighted that for me.

* * *

We somehow managed to park up somewhere around the back streets of central London. It was busy and took us what felt like an hour. But we found a place to stop and I was glad to finally get out the car and away from the land lady's constant crunching on cereal bars. Mrs Singh insisted that we all carry some part of the picnic, with her of course taking charge of the picnic mother ship.

The miracle of joy that had befallen the Singh household that morning vanished somewhere on the way.

I guessed this was mainly to do with the heavy traffic jams and excited revellers in herd-like droves that were encountered on the way. The usual cloud of mundane and moody normality fell over us once again as we walked laden with food. Ruby was her normal sullen self and the happy couple were bickering about whether to stop and begin on the food—one thing for sure it would have lightened the loads we carried. Like when would we actually get to eat something? I was famished and mentally promised myself that I would give in and go get a burger—There were fast food joints on every corner in London, so as you could imagine there were a lot!

The crowds that were walking through Victoria Street were immense, rowdy as thousands trundled along the pathways—this had to be a human version of an elephant stampede.

"It don't look like Buckingham Palace to me! Are you sure we are going in the right direction?"

Ruby's growing cheekiness didn't help the growing frustration that we all felt.

"Relax just follow the crowds! They know where to go!"

Mr Singh came out with the only rational thing any of us had heard all day up until that point. We followed the crowds, like we had a choice! It was more like we were pushed along with the tide.

But even so it was the common sense thing to do. The quiet man was a genius! The exquisite smell of frying hot dogs and fried onions filled the air, no longer prepared to wait my stomach lurched and demanded immediate attention. Within seconds I gave into the sizzling temptation. The onions were still frying as they lay deliciously across the top of the bread roll and meat that lay within it. I salivated in sheer desire at the image of the hotdog that I held in my hand. The other fumbling inside my purse for the change I needed. The gruff looking man looked impatient, me too as I longed to take that first bite.

". . . Erm, what about me?"

I paid for the second hot dog, Ruby too was not happy about the tight control her mother had on the food. I watched her gulp down her hot dog within about a minute. I was indeed flattered now that I had a follower but there also was the worry there that she may inherit my 'tyres'. These came from an excess of over indulgence, it had accumulated over the years to form part of my physical landscape. These 'spare parts' showed no signs of going anywhere. As we ate the two of us could not have been more silent in the middle of the royal wedding induced maelstrom. Neither of us made little more than a loud munching sound.

Before one could ask 'Does one fancy a fondant fancy' there we were at Westminster Abbey itself!

Everyone seemed to be wearing plush hats in the shape of crowns. Were the royal family aware of this? If I was one of the royals I would so have these things outlawed! They were hideous and vulgar. Where had the great British sense of style gone? This was the sort of thing that Vogue and Glamour would have cringed at.

Luckily my own cringing was interrupted by Ruby's screams.

"Oh my God I can see her she is coming over!"

There was no way with all the people there that she could have seen absolutely anything! She was over reacting again, all one had to do was to look up at the giant television screens that were set up high on some of the buildings. Early afternoon by that point we had missed the main ceremony. My hand was grabbed and pulled into the crowds feeling like a small fish in a big tin of sardines. I could hardly breathe but Ruby pulled me in even deeper right into the thick of it.

"She's there! Look! And look there are camera's everywhere!"

Ruby smiled her superstar smile that only ever came out when she got her own way. But highlight of the day so far for me was seeing a corner of the stunning wedding dress, white and intricately detailed it was one of the most beautiful things I have ever seen in my life. . .

"It's her! It's really her!"

The new Duchess glowed brightly as there was the fleeting glimpse of her radiant face. Flawless all eyes were on her. It was no wonder she was radiating happiness her dreams had come true and she had just married her prince. I looked up at the giant screens that were on display above the crowds. We were in the presence of a real princess, too beautiful for words I and everyone else that day had totally fallen in love with the stunning young woman. Her radiant smile, those dark sultry eyes and long chestnut hair, she was perfection in human form.

Our new princess was every inch the beauty that the nation had wanted for their beloved Prince. (Yes I know get the violins out, but this was a truly emotional experience)

"Come on! We can get closer!"

Ruby squeezed my hand even tighter as we pushed through to the metal barrier, soon we found ourselves at the core. Flashing lights, the thousands of cameras hurt my eyes as they flickered ceaselessly. Positioned between the cold metal and a large man with the world's biggest beer belly, I could think of a few places I would rather have been. He was the sort of man who would claim that his lump was in actual fact pure muscle and be fairly proud about it. I could tell you from where I was standing this really was not anywhere near muscle! Firstly it was soft and gurgled loudly, so I used my limited knowledge of the human body, and lovely six packs on male calendar models.

My heart beat wildly while I watched on, then before I knew it:

"Catherine!"

I screamed at the top of my lungs so hard that my chest hurt. The blood rushed to my head knowing that one was so close to royalty! Closer than possibly than every generation of my family have ever been to them, my mother would really have been insane with jealousy if she knew where I had been! Every inch of my tingled in anticipation, even though I was wedged in between a fat man and a cold hard steel place, this was truly a fantastic feeling. I could tell the grandchildren about this over a roaring fire, and watch their chubby red cheeked faces look upon me in angelic adoration. Yes I Ophelia of the Strainge's was here and a part of history!

Then my worst nightmare happened, but a nightmare that somehow became a blessing in disguise! Well you remember the pain I had wearing the peep toe shoes that I had so enthusiastically donned that morning? Now the reality was screaming that I really should have opted for something flat with steel toe caps. Mr big beer belly stamped his one very large doc marten wearing foot onto my fragile toes. The pain shot straight through to my core as every cell screeched out in a high pitched silence. No sound was released apart from breath, the pain caused me to hit a pitch I not in the average

human being's hearing range. Each blood vessel in my body threatened to explode there and then, but they didn't and I counted myself extremely lucky to have not spontaneously combusted on the spot.
What happened next would go down in history as one of my greatest moments ever; in fact I would be so bold as to say this was my most memorable achievement.
As I was saying with the insurmountable pain I let out a roar that hit decibels not previously deemed possible to emit, but then it became louder. The crowd around me stopped what they had been doing a Nano second later.
Ceasing to munch on their hot dogs and burgers, halting their cheers instead it felt as if everyone outside Westminster Abbey turned to see where this pained scream had come from. But imagine this amazing thing if you can! The stunning bride looked over in my direction, her beautiful eyes hovered over Ruby and I for the briefest of seconds before she got on with the crowd greetings. The noise levels in returned as promptly as they had halted. Things got back to normal but not for me or Ruby who like me was now in total awe.
"Sorry love!"
Beer belly man apologised, the age of chivalry was truly alive and kicking which was nice. I should have thanked him for stamping as hard as he possibly could on my now mangled peep toe shoe. Yes I would no doubt go home to find that my every bone in my foot has been dislocated but never mind about all that! I was blessed from that moment onwards. That didn't matter; nothing did anymore apart from this. This was my claim to fame there had to be a few camera's that had taken a shot of me!
"Ophelia! Ruby!"
The familiar voices recognised, we had left them a while back so obviously they were concerned. Ruby and I made our way to the worried calls.
"Wow you! I can't believe it!"
Ruby was my number one fan! There was no way I would ever shake her off now. She worshipped me and grinned at me in adoration all the way home.

I'm now writing from my bedroom, I have my feet in a steaming hot bucket of water and I am attempting to peel each toe out from the crumpled up mess that have become my feet. The legend that are the peep toe shoes are in the corner of my room, some of the sequins have been scrapped off from one shoe with the force of the beer belly man's blow. They have now been truly broken into but I don't think they are road worthy. They are too precious for that! From now on they will be a museum piece. There is the chance that someone had filmed me screeching in agony and I will be an internet legend myself. In which case I will have to keep these shoes safe, they may be highly sought after some day. But for the time being what a total souvenir of a totally epic day that will truly live on for me in total infamy!

Friday 6th May
Amanda's leaving do

The great lady herself has literally left the building and surprisingly I was quite sad about it. After months of petty library-related squabbles I was finally back in a good emotional—she goes and pulls a stunt like this! She announced it at the last staff meeting a week ago.
"I'm leaving it's my time to retire!"
We all knew it was on the cards in the next few years, but she decided to go early for some reason. Sebastian was dying to find out what this reason was, but she gave nothing away! All the long running feuds that we have been involved in seem to have gone out of the window. She seems at ease with the world and is actually happy for the first time in a zillion years. I don't quite know what to make of this new and free Amanda! And I . . . well . . . I . . . Feel a little let down.
Who am I going to moan about with Sebastian now? Memories of our raging arguments about reserved books floated through my sad mind like a butterfly flitting past on a warm summer's

day. There was always Lucy but she was more the type to talk behind one's back and not put up a good argument.

My philosophical thought for the decade is this—We all have to leave one day and as sad as that is, it's the truth and today had been Amanda's final day at work. Despite her letting me down I wished her well. From snippets of a conversation that I eaves dropped on, I knew that she had planned a holiday to St Kitts in the Caribbean and was intending on finding herself a nice young man to be her companion. Perhaps she had a secret lover out there?

In the usual style the remaining members of the team joined and put a collection together. What does a person get the lady with the worst fashion tastes ever? A pair of vintage retro earrings and sort of matching handbag, one that was picked up at a more 'upper class' second hand fashion boutique. Sebastian although sometimes a pain was a lifesaver in cases such as these, the rest of us were grateful for his efforts. . .

She was suitably impressed with her gifts and even more so when their buyer reassured her that they were 'very' vintage designer wear. She lapped it up and as expected enjoyed being the centre of attention. There was to be a lot more of that later on at her leaving do, Amanda really was queen for a night. I half expected Lucy and Sebastian to have organised strippers the way they both carried on about the 'big surprise!'

So it came to be that I was stuck in the middle of pinky and perky (AKA Lucy and Amanda). There was the four of us there in the middle of deepest darkest Essex in rather a nice pub style restaurant. The Nut and Squirrel (or was it the other way round? I can't remember) had a lovely country inn style atmosphere. The lovely Olde Worlde style décor combined with my rum and coke were the only thing that kept me sane after the drive there. It had been a disastrous one with the 'short-cut' costing us an extra half an hour so. Sebastian and I had arrived fashionably late to the two sour faced and non-impressed librarians.

"So are you planning on staying a Library Assistant?"

Lucy wasn't enjoying the awkward silence either, one that signified a teetotal library leaving do.

"Erm yes"

This was a good question I hadn't really thought about my career I was far too busy working to do that. What I didn't expect was Lucy to come at me with a weird sort of snarled approval.

"I was a Library assistant for years! And it hasn't done me any harm!"

I watched my arch nemesis as her wrinkled top lip sucked on the straw of her drink. Sebastian had caught the end of the comment from Lucy, coming back from the gents.

"Yes what are your plans for the future Ophelia? Are you going for that promotion?"

"I . . . am not sure right now . . ."

"But surely you would have some kind of career path carved out by now . . . I mean you're no spring chicken are you!"

This was harsh but it hit home—Thank you Sebastian! Before I had time to answer my body was hauled up by the wrists and over to the bar by Sebastian.

"Come on it's our round! Besides I want to tell you about the 'surprise' you are not going to believe it but first things first!"

I hated the way I instantly became his rag doll when it came to buying drinks but tres excitemont when it came to this 'big surprise'. I knew he had got a male stripper in for Amanda. It had to be!

It was the usual for everyone else and rum and coke for me, there seemed to be a lot more rum in the last drink I had. But there was not a complaint in sight, this party needed livening up and fast before we all turned to stone, I prayed inwardly for this 'miracle' to occur.

The stripy body con dress chosen for the occasion wasn't the greatest idea on the planet but at least I looked like I was trying. It was better to be seen having a go than to not have bothered at all right? Especially when it came to fashion! I looked over in horror at Sebastian who slumped over the bar, he screeched and waved down the barmaid like she was a cab. The barmaid in turn clearly fought the urge to roll her eyes at his aggressive command; clearly she dealt with Sebastian's all day long!

* * *

"Hello there!"
The suave sophisticated voice came out of nowhere and belonged to a shadow, a big giant shadow behind the murky mists. A first glance it had the shape of a monster. But they didn't frequent pubs surely! It had to just be a big grizzly beer bellied pub goer. But the voice was far too sophisticated to belong to someone like the lout that stepped on my foot (which I was still recovering from)
This could have been a scene straight out of a horror movie or thriller, although it wasn't that thrilling. The foggy haze cleared to reveal more of the dark shadowy figure that stood menacingly before me. There was a short confused pause as I squinted trying to make out who or what was speaking to me. That rum and coke certainly did get into the blood stream much quicker than I had expected, I obviously couldn't hold my drink any longer now that I approached old age!
"Hi I'm Tim . . ."
Sebastian flung over my second drink to the section of the bar I slouched casually against. He could have been doing a 'Tom Cruise in Cocktail' impression. I took one blasé sip and watched this man. There he stood like something mysterious that had just emerged from a cold damp cave. I couldn't quite put my finger on it but there was something vaguely sea-monster about him. His big hairy forearm reached forwards with a hand that must have been three times the size of mine, it was out and ready to greet me.
"I'm Tim!"
The voice turned gruff as I waited in the drink induced daze, he was impatient at my slow reaction to his warm welcoming one. The fat hairy hand had enough and grabbed my thin one but I pulled back. This was a strange way of getting to know someone and I certainly didn't appreciate his 'forwardness' on this occasion.
"That's nice Tim but why should I be interested in who you are?"
Minus the Rum and Coke's there was no way I would have had anywhere near as much bravery as I had that evening. The inner

hormonal woman had just emerged and she wasn't taking any nonsense.

"Erm... Excuse me?"

I told another sip of the drink and propped myself up against the bar. I continued to survey this man from head to toe.

"... You heard me! I want to know why it is soooo important that I know that you are Tim."

His tweed jacket was ill fitting, the leather elbow patches were worn from probably many an evening with his arms on a pub table obviously talking to 'young' ladies. The dark greying hair and heavy thick eyebrows over his dark eyes made him look perhaps more sinister and mysterious than was normal. His shoes were the thing that stuck out the most, black and white spats with bright red socks. Quirky and cute on a leggy eighteen year old supermodel but not so on a forty something year old man. Where did he get his fashion sense from... Mars?

Did he do this sort of thing often? Well it certainly seemed that way with the brazen attitude he had, demanding to tell me who he was.

"So I take it you are part of the gang then?"

He nodded over in the direction of the prune faced women perched in the darkest corner of the pub. This really was far too much and he had clearly over stepped the mark with me. This man needed to be put in his place and that that moment I felt that I was the woman to do it.

"Yeah and what if I am?"

I sniffed indignantly pulling down the too tight stripy number. I wished desperately that I had opted for my jeans with a t-shirt and cardigan, it would have been easier to kung-fu/karate chop this man in a more practical outfit.

"... Well I just thought I'd come over to introduce myself"

"Into that sort of thing are you, Librarians? Cardigans and pencil skirts? Hey? Come on you can tell me!"

The man in front of me shuffled back totally indignant at what I was saying.

"Look thank you Mr Tim but I'm really not very interested I'm here with my friends for a quiet drink that's all so if you wouldn't mind terribly jogging on!"

Sebastian came over frantic; this struck me as weird through my growing alcohol induced haze.

"Sebastian this is Tim! He's got a thing for ladies who work in a Library!"

Sebastian grabbed me by the shoulder and pulled me close enough to whisper hard to me.

"No Ophelia! He's the big surprise I was telling you about!"

He turned to the big scary man and looked all apologetic.

"Tim I'm so sorry, she's had a few . . ."

He made a drinking cup sign with his hands.

"That's quite alright don't worry"

Tim held up his hands and smiled as warmly as a man could who had just been insulted only moments ago. Why was Sebastian being nice to him? He was hideous!

"You mean you know this man! Has he tried his luck with you too?"

Sebastian sighed as the hulking mass of a man did his very best to hold back the obvious rage that was building up and threatening to burst. He basically wanted to throttle me it was in his eyes.

"Ophelia this is Tim; he's taking over from Amanda as our new branch manager"

Who would have thought that one could be as sober as a judge in a millisecond?

"Oh hello there Mr Tim . . . I mean Tim . . . Is it ok if I call you Tim?"

"Yes its fine"

He replied through hard as concrete clenched jaws with the remnants of the low growl he had let out previously. Sebastian pushed me aside and was even more apologetic to Frankenstein's monster. I wanted to be sick! How could he betray me? I thought he was *my* friend! But he was doing his best to cool tempers and it worked.

"Yes Ophelia and I were just saying how much we would like you to join us for a drink! What do you say?"

The very angry giant Tim agreed despite not looking impressed. I felt that this evening had been the beginning of the end! My career in local government seemed to snowball from this moment onwards. I would have to do absolutely everything to get back into his good books, foot massages in the office at lunchtime, constant coffee making and offering to run his elderly mother to the shops to do her shopping for her. I'd possibly have to also sew back the elbow patches onto his jacket arms; I inwardly gagged at this thought.

All I had to do now was to keep quiet and keep smiling for the rest of the evening. I couldn't jeopardise any future I had by inflaming the situation further. The silence was deafening and I was so desperately pleased when Lucy blurted out the next topic of conversation:

"So facial piercings—yes to freedom of expression or a definite no?"

Tim brought his drink over and sat down his expression was still one of thunder. But one consoled oneself with the thought that this could have been his usual expression.

"But why would someone want to go through the pain?"

Amanda had obviously not thought much of her replacement and dismissed him in a style that only she could do.

"I've heard there's one called a 'Monroe' but Marilyn didn't have any facial piercings!"

"Maybe she had them somewhere else?"

"Never mind about all that, who else is going to buy me another goodbye drink?"

Sebastian looked away at the walls pretending to be interested in the mull coloured wall décor.

The thought of seeing my boss rather tipsy was tempting and it would be worth spending my meagre salary to see it.

Everything on the gold embossed cover of the menu was extortionately priced! I wished I had taken the hint from Sebastian. While the rest of the group seemed to be busy on the topic of body modification Tim stared hard. He watched me like a hawk and made me feel like it wouldn't be long until my library career ended. The low growl returned but no one else noticed. Was I imagining it? Did this man think he was a werewolf or a fictional monster of the night? Was it the drink? One thing that I am under no illusion about is that this man does not like me, and now I'm in for it!

Tuesday 10th May
This year's get away

Even after last year's fiasco in Istanbul that had left me scarred for life, I have somewhat reluctantly agreed to go on holiday once again with Seraphina. 'Why?' I hear you all cry. Well apart from the annoying spawn of the dark one kicking my plane seat all the way to Turkey, later being left alone to shower all my woes onto Claude the barman (who is now incidentally my new BFF) I actually quite enjoyed it all.

The choice to go was based upon a few contributing factors. Well firstly my spending this year has spiralled out of control, as a result I have opted to be better with the little cash that I do have. A cheap holiday is preferable than having none and spending the summer at work with a zillion zitty school children. In past years I have been emotionally blackmailed into doing their homework. One time I got a tale that really pulled on the heart strings. She couldn't do her homework because her little sister had flushed it down the toilet, if she doesn't complete it before the school term starts then she wasn't allowed to go to prom. She had spent a whole year designing the dress she would hopefully be wearing and had saved up her pocket money for it.

It truly brought tears to my eyes, the thought of not experiencing that one night that epitomises coming-of-age! That first real drinking session! Throwing up behind the bandstand and then walking up to the class hunk and snogging him with puke breath. I simply had to make sure she went! Spending six weeks writing her GCSE Coursework was not my idea of fun summer. No I would rather be on a club18-30's to Ibiza—and that's really saying something!

Seraphina put an interesting proposition to me earlier today. She had another one of her ideas—normally it would have been followed by groans and flat out refusal. Not this time—there was no groaning because I actually quite like the idea, yes it's a little different but this could potentially be a great break from it all. Heaven knows that I need it.

Sankthansaften is the Norwegian for Midsummers day or night. This happens all over northern Europe every year around the 23rd of June. I did some Google searching as one does and found out that amidst some Pagan celebrations, huge bonfires will be lit across the coast. According to Seraphina it is quite a euphoric experience and one that she said I would remember for the rest of my life (and I believe it)

I sincerely hope the 'unforgettable' part is in a good way and not a horror-filled one. She plans on getting us there by road, instantly that will be nice and cheap right? Either this or we will be hitching rides with big ugly looking juggernaut drivers. I shudder at this thought! I thought of all the things we could be making our way to Norway in. A caravan would be lovely as I would be able to pop off every so often and make Seraphina another cup of extremely strong coffee which will help her stay awake. Not the healthiest option but a necessary one as she will be doing the driving (it may not be the best of options me driving as I have a mere provisional license, and I don't want to be arrested)

Another concern is that this journey would clock up a lot more carbon air miles adding to a massive polluted foot print type thing. This in turn would cause an even greyer patch in the Earth's atmosphere. But according to her that's not the point; it's a road trip and will totally add to the holiday experience.

While this all sounds great, here's the big question: Could Seraphina and I cope with each other for the time we are together? How long would it be before we tore each other's hair out? Or worse kill each other! In the middle of nowhere there would be no one to stop us from naked lady mud wrestling to the absolute death! It would be a two woman version of Golding's 'Lord of the Flies'. This was a scary thought. On the other hand I loved it in a sort of Thelma and Louise way, two women of the world getting away from it all, and going somewhere no one knew us with the real hope of beginning again! My take on it all is that this is going to be a pilgrimage style holiday, a spiritual journey into the unknown heart of Europe (which probably isn't that mysterious really) and would be well worth going on. According to her 'I will be a renewed soul' but the time it was all over. This is great! Yes! I really need a bit of renewing at the moment. We are going to Sankthansaften wotsit!

Monday 30th May
Stalking tendencies resurface

Am I going crazy or actually turning into a real live stalker? Most probably but I haven't seen Cole—the extremely lovely but mysterious man next door since hijacking him on New Year's Eve.
The now infamous blue and white split screen Campervan that is normally parked outside his home next door is nowhere to be seen. Not that I am actually stalking him but it hasn't been there for a while. I had sort of gotten used to seeing it parked outside every time I left to go to work. But never fear and don't worry dear readers I have no plans to go through his bins again. No it is now fully understood that this is illegal and sometimes may cause bad feeling to come in-between an otherwise flourishing friendship. No there was nothing for it but to just accept that the gorgeous man himself is not in residence.
But the mind still wanders it can't help itself, just what has happened to him? You may have guessed by now through previous diary entries that one has a little bit of a crush on him. Every time walk out of the Singh's front door, a quick fluttering of butterflies occurs. I have tried deep breathing, just ignoring my feelings and even looking the other way but nothing seems to work.
Each time I walk past his over grown front garden (which was most days seeing as he is only next door) the thought flashes through my mind without fail: 'Is he there?'
The strong temptation to walk up the uneven path to his front door has often threatened to overwhelm me, but what would I say?
"Hi how are you just wanted to check that you are still alive because I actually quite like you? And yes you are so I'll go now Goodbye!"

That really is borderline stalking along with pressing my face up and licking his painted window frames. One simply had to reign oneself in! He may have found himself a lovely lady to spend his time with on a sunny beach somewhere; Cole could be tanning that lovely muscular body of his. I wasn't sure he was that muscular but I'm sure underneath the shirt his trim body was fairly buff. Perhaps the reason he wasn't there could have been something much more down to earth like he had found a job elsewhere and worked away from home a lot more. I found myself unnaturally worried for this alluring stranger.
"So you are interested in him then?"
Mrs Singh was in her abode (the kitchen) and eternally cooking which was normal. The floral apron that was covered in pinks and reds caught my eye and almost hypnotised me as I watched her dart about picking up ingredients to go into the pot.
"I could tell that from New Year's day!"
It was frustrating how the land lady didn't miss a single thing. While this was a very admiral quality in most cases, in this one I wished that my feelings were not so obvious—it was embarrassing! After all I didn't want her to notice my cheeks flush whenever she mentioned him. Or the fact that I stumbled over every word when talking about him, that was a real give away! Mrs Singh only grinned whenever the subject came up over the kitchen table. If it were my mother things would have been very different, she would have disapproved instantly. He was a 'creative' type and she didn't want one of those as part of the family!
"He's ok"
"Just ok? Are you sure?"
I involuntarily let out the biggest most glorious smile known to mankind, so wide that it hurt my face. My mind went back to that morning after the night before, how I stumbled back into the flat. My mascara was in places it really shouldn't have been with a long hot shower on the agenda remedied this in no time. I had the same grin on my face as I had all these months later. I'm sure that this was meant to be a good sign right?

Sunday 5th June
My Trip in the Geisha Wedges

My feet are only really just recovering from the peep toe incident. It's taken a while but they have gotten there. Finally I am able to walk in a straight line which is always good thing to do. I was now ready to take on the challenge I promised to do ages ago. Partly thinking that perhaps the wedges should be left in their in their still pristine box. After all they really didn't need to be worn; they are a work of shoe art. So one would be completely forgiven for leaving them be. However after being indirectly challenged buy the land lady making her opinion known about my purchase things were different. I had wanted to challenge her ever since and would so prove her wrong. The brave decision to wear my Geisha wedges was made this morning; it was an 'on the spur of the moment' thing. What was the worst that could happen? I could fall from towering heights and break every bone, the plus side is that this would mean at least a year off work! These wedges were mine and it would be even more of a shame if they never saw the light of day!

The staircase had been tackled successfully, ok so it was only from my room to the ground floor and then back again. But that was still a whole forty something steps with only one hand holding the bannister!

It was a case of slow and steady won the race despite Ruby and her school friends running up the stairs alongside me walking down it. They found it extremely funny that I was stomping at a snail's pace and called me 'grandma' on several occasions. Which was not amusing and only served to spur me on urging me to be even faster. I would train these feet to love the wedges so much that walking in them would soon become second nature. Anyway by the time the two rounds of the staircase and the kitchen had been completed, I decided to clomp my way through the park as I was ready! Meteorologically speaking there is no more ice and the ground is dry enough to be considered safe walking ground. What the heck I was going to risk it! Everything made for perfect circumstances to road test my fantastic beauties!

A short distance away the park was more of an old patch of summer scorched land that never really returned to its former glory. I wore a pair of scruffy old trainers there with the wedges in my holdall. A comfortable start was preferable; I didn't fancy negotiating an obstacle course just to get there! The closest park bench was located yards away from the entrance gates; this was an awesome place to start so I parked myself there. The wedges came out of my back pack and went onto my feet as soon as I flicked off the grubby old trainers. They slipped right on; this must have been what Cinderella felt like! It was all or nothing from that moment onwards. If I failed I would feel like a fashion reject for the rest of my life.

How could I possibly get anywhere if I couldn't even wear a pair of heels? There was no way any respectable fashion magazine or online boutique would ever take me or my work seriously, being forever known as the one that can't walk in heels!

The main pathway in front of me was my fashion runway! And I was going to walk it like I owned it! The park was mine this Sunday! Perfect terrain for the United nude Geisha shoes to tread on, there was absolutely nothing stopping me except for pure undiluted fear!

I stood up on the stilt-like shoes. Once again just like in the department store I could see everything, from the tops of the bushes to some of the picnicking mums in the park with their toddlers.

A group of older kids flashed past on bikes, screeching and howling at each other. Why couldn't they just have walked like everyone else? They cycled so fast and nearly sent me wobbling, darn those pesky kids with their bicycles!

I waved my clenched fist at one of them like an angry pensioner would! They laughed in response, how dare they? My angered reaction must have made it extremely funny, perhaps they were laughing at the wedges? Well what did they know about fashion? With their smelly old retro t-shirts and baggy jeans! They rode off further into the distance laughing. Boo to the younger generation for making me feel my age! But the main thing was that they were gone and I could continue on my catwalk. I walked tall and was almost as tall as the trees. Was this the world that super svelte models faced every day?

Yes yes yes it was and I could see absolutely everything. One step after another and I was doing it! This walking in heels wasn't so hard after all. My victory lap was made so much better by the tiny little girl below me who I had to squint to see. She must have been about five years old and wore a very cute pink frilly dress, talk about Barbie overload!

"I like your shoes!"

She took a messy bite of the massive ice-cream she held in her hand and looked up at me with a messy smile. Her worried mother trundled over and picked up the girl.

"I'm so sorry"

She started wide eyed up at me too and then dropped a glance back to the wedges. Mum really didn't have a clue as to what to make of me. For mums it's all about jogging bottoms and sweat shirts. Shoes must be ultra-comfortable with all that running about!

"It's fine really!"

The mother smiled with a squirming child in her arms, she half walked and half sprinted away from me to the group of other mums by the lake. Would no doubt be sneered at behind my back for not getting involved in messy motherhood like they had done!

Triumphant at my still standing posture, I felt in a strange way that I had won over the public even if this 'public' consisted of a small child. Continuing to walk through the park I gazed down regally at each person that passed me. This excursion had been super great! Next step the high street and then maybe Bond Street? Mayfair? Central London could very well be my Oyster! There would be many more fans there!

The next bench was in view, I had proven my point so slumped on the wooden seat. Mrs Singh would be impressed I was sure of it! Just a little more practice but for then I was happy to flip the wedges off my feet and rub my toes in the cool soft grass.

Friday 10th June
Kaftans and beads!

Ah the Great Summer Festival, an institution to rival any other. The chance for thousands to get together for a week or so, live in tents and roll around in mud! What better way to spend the summer than to do these very things? A change of scenery is what is on the cards and Sankthansaften is according to Seraphina 'the event of the year'. This is really well needed especially after Amanda's leaving do. Maybe Tim would completely forget everything that happened? A clean slate would be perfect! I wouldn't be so worried about my job any longer. There are only a few more 'awkward' days left until we leave. The plan now is to just keep my head down, mouth shut and hope for the best. Pretty much the same as I had been doing since the night of the do.

There was something very liberating in the thought of not having to bother with looking flawless or washing even. There's no knowing if there will even be facilities to wash, or if there was even any point in taking soap or toilet roll with me. So I won't bother and instead will rely on the power of prayer to protect me from any horrendous infections. I can't afford to take time off from work being ill with something very tropical. If another head was grown beside my own I would just have to go in to work and brace myself for the reaction. There was no guessing what the great East London public would make of my new look. On second thoughts maybe that would be a good thing and may help matters—Two heads are better than on (sorry).

I began packing for the holiday a week ago. One of the items that had to be taken was my large floppy sun hat, one that would hide all the signs of grime that my hair would accumulate in its unwashed state. I would be most likely be slumming it in foot deep in mud for most of the time there. Other items that went into the tatty old suitcases included my prized floral wellingtons, sequinned hot pants a la Kylie Minogue but mine were neon pink and even shinier (if that was possible). These with fishnets and one of the many skimpy vest tops I had packed were going to be staple part of my festival wardrobe.

Each day the excitement grows, by the time we do actually leave for the festival I will probably spontaneously erupt with the anticipation. However there is a major dilemma as always and it's this: What does a thirty something library assistant wear to such an event? How can one be cool without doing an Amanda and looking like mutton dressed as lamb? Fashion is a serious business despite the deceptiveness of the mud covered thousands that attend these things. Unofficial prizes go to the most bizarre costumed attendees or the most outlandish looking folk in even fashion category. Big bright and bold seem to be the order of the day.

But this is no Cocktail bar where one could quite easily get away with anything that looks sharp and body hugging. Frowned upon would be fitted body con dresses and thick eyeliner giving one maximum impact in a dark and crowded bar. I could prepare for those sorts of events without even blinking a mascaraed eyelid! My wardrobe was brimming full with variations on that 'little black dress'.

Making a bold statement in the middle of a muddy field in broad harsh daylight would be a whole different scenario. But as you all know I am a girl who likes a fashion challenge!

Partly one wonders if one can get away with 'anti rebelling' and attend the Sankthansaften in my work gear. The favourite knee skimming pencil skirt with cream coloured blouse, but with a twist! I would add to it with some glittery nail polish or some far out neon earrings?

'Normal' at a festival would be looking like summers pin up girls Sienna Miller and Kate Moss. The boho look mainly consists of: Long wispy hair sometimes crowned with a daisy chain-like tiara or some kind of flower inspired head dress. This would be teamed with a long floral maxi dress and bangles/ beaded bracelets all the way from wrist to elbow. This is the general idea that the high streets have been banging on about ever since these two glamorous ladies championed the look five or six years ago.

Bohemian chic has been around for a lot longer than that however, I'm sure since the nineteen seventies. Although in recent years other items of clothing have been incorporated into this look. Think tight fitting shorts and boob tubes, this is more of a neo-festival look.

So I will aim for floral prints with the odd quirky item of clothing. Festivals are about making fools of ourselves so that's what needs to be done in order to fit in. Call me an old stick in the mud but there has to be some level of decorum on my part at Sankthansaften. There's no way I will be prancing around stark naked in the middle of nowhere.

My floral wellies that were brought two years ago, I found these little gems in an Aldgate East market. These lovely things caught my eye as I passed them. The stall that the boots were sitting on was also full of knick knacks, alarm clocks and egg timers along with plastic bouquets of flowers. The bright blue boots covered in a pink and red rose print stuck out like a sore thumb and screamed out to me. They were so unusual and I loved them instantly, the boots had wanted me to be their owner.

They were a brilliantly perfect copy of a more well-known brand only a lot cheaper! Finding them was a total win win situation! The boots would be mine for a reasonable price and the market trader who sold them could stop shouting for a moment while I paid for them. I had to have them there was simply no choice, so as per usual with zero resistance I let rip with the cash. But it always feels better when you get hold of that bargain! Before you all judge me please remember that I live on a meagre wage and trying to be as 'in' as possible takes some careful planning with funds. Contrary to what it may seem like—I do not spend my time and all my cash on shoes.

As I paid up I envisioned gallivanting across fields wearing them. One could so see oneself mucking out stables ruddy cheeked and smiling! These were a far cry from the boring racing green ones that have been worn for millennia by many a countryman or woman. However since the day I bought them home in their brown paper bag I haven't worn them at all. These quickly became a part of the mass of clothing and accessories that have been hoarded. The blue and pink rubber boots have sat at the front of my main wardrobe; they greet me every time I open the wardrobe doors to get ready. They meekly smile at me with each opening, hoping that each day would bring them a chance. A mere glint of hope when they could get up and run free at long last, I looked back at them sadly as there was never any opportunity for them to explore the big wide world.

I put it down to them being just so extremely lovely, too lovely in fact. Perish the thought of wearing them in the garden to help Mrs Singh do the weeding! Covered in mud? I don't think so! I wanted my flawless boots to stay that pristine.

But fate it seems has thankfully intervened and now they have the chance, they have waited for the whole of their little rubber lives for this moment. They are coming with me to the festival! It instantly ticks a big 'floral' box for festival wear.

So that's one 'cool' thing to start with. Trying to be economical is what it's all about when it comes to my packing. There is really no point in spending a packet on new clothes and accessories that I am really only going to wear once or maybe at a push twice. So I am forced to look even deeper into the mountain of things I have collected.

On a lighter note I do have some hot pink glittery hot pants. Now the last time I wore these was a few years ago at a friend's party. I was svelte (yes I know hard to believe) and felt amazing in them—it didn't matter that most of the people there thought this was a mega fashion fail. The fact of the matter was that I looked slim and was able to slink my way into them with my then almost non-existent waist. So powerful was this glorious feeling that I vowed to never ever give these beauties to the charity shop or lend them to anyone else ever!

They will sit with my prized belongings and be a type of trophy that I could one 'fat' day boast about. We all know that sooner or later that muffin top will inevitably grow in size; it's a fact of life. The hot pants would in a way be a snap shot of the past the way high school photographs are. No one ever seems to like their old childhood photographs but the thing is that these same people will realise much later that they looked their best in them. Unless you are Sean Connery and you just get better with age.

My future self would screech at teenagers as they throw stones at my house on the way home from school. I'd wave my clenched fists at them and claim loudly something like:

"... When I was your age I was skinny too!"

I would hold out the pink glittery number and wave it out into the open so that everyone and their dog could see them. No one would miss them for miles around, they and I will one day be infamous!

The wildest thing in the wardrobe I will have to take them with the floral boots, what a super combination they would make! Now all I had to do was find them. Once I did and managed to squeeze into them (this would be a struggle at first), the chances are that no one else will really be too offended at the sight of me. The festival goers will no doubt be too busy trying to make their own garish fashion statements. So wild and wacky that fashion bloggers will photograph them and write out their outlandish outfits.

Determined to be one of the weirdest looking people at the Sankthansaften I've decided to look through all of Missy's hiding places first, bearing in mind all that had happened last year.

Although she seems to have matured since then and now prefers to curl up and sleep under my bed rather than clawing through everything. In case I have neglected to mention or you haven't read the prequel to this book—Missy is Mrs Singh's cat and usually is up to mischief. Despite this she is very much loved. Finding her asleep on my precious Ted Baker jeans one time was extremely endearing, like Ruby she is a cat who knows her fashion! (Although Missy is an actual cat, Ruby is a human most of the time) However I can't let her drag expensive or important items of clothing to dark corners of the garden. In a nutshell, Missy dashed off with an expensive bikini and dragged it out into the garden where it stayed for months festering. As you can imagine I was none too pleased and have vowed to find the hot pants. It will not be their fate to be left behind the garden shed! Oh No! Mark my words I will find them!

* * *

After my last update with real fire in my belly I did as promised and turned the whole house upside down! Determination was the word of the day as I flew around my bedroom looking for even a corner of pink glitter. Even something that would give me a clue as to where they could be found!
I even did a 'when was the last time the hot pants were seen?' thing. Anyway I found it in a very unlikely place!
Is there any explanation as to why it was in the Singh's household's laundry basket? It's a big plastic basket that usually appears between the kitchen and living room on Friday's when it was housework/laundry day. Well lo and behold there it was as clear as day! And it looked like it had been worn! I gasped in horror as I pulled it out of the basket to examine them. How could this be? All this time I had thought they were in the furthest reaches of my wardrobe. No they had a secret life being worn by the Land lady of all people. I'm now up in my room having pant napped my own hot pants—counting each and every sequin on them! My poor babies! What was she doing wearing them? Please let this be some horrendous nightmare.

Saturday 18th June
The Message

Literally a day before we leave for Norway and he does this to me! He called, yes Neville finally got in touch after months. He left me a voicemail! I virtually kicked myself for not having my phone in my hand with my volume turned up to the max. Up to ghetto blaster volume would have done it, this probably would have ensured that his call was picked up. I had so many questions to ask him like:
'I thought you were dead where have you been? If you are really that disgusted with my fashion sense why did you just not say and we could have ended it? Why did you have to keep the hope alive for all this time? What are you some kind of sick

weirdo who gets off on this kind of thing? Are you a serial love rat and have another five girls or more on the go?'

The silence has been unbearable. I was totally speechless when his number flashed across my phone's screen. Just what was he playing at? Holding my breath I listened to the message that he left.

"Hi Ophelia, Hope you are fine, listen I need to talk to you. It's fairly urgent, there are a few things you need to know, call me back"

I listened to the message again and again, analysis everything about it, each word, the tone of his voice. Even every millisecond of background noise was mentally made a note of.

The call sounded as if it was made next to a dual carriageway. There were car horns going off right left and centre in the background. My mind flitted around wondering what was going on when he made the call. I listened again, and then again. As desperate as I was not to admit it, hanging on to his every word came easy to me. The smooth voice that I longed to hear sounded concerned. An eagle eyed Lucy watched me from across the staff room during the lunch break. I could see she was trying to work out what I was listening too; her bespectacled gaze was fixed on my concentrated expression. She had never seen me in such a state before, it was a strange 'state' to be in somewhere between ecstatic and furious. There were almost tears of angry joy after all this time.

Ok so first things first "Hope you are fine . . ." No I certainly wasn't! Then: " . . . listen I need to talk to you. It's fairly urgent". It had to be something seriously dire for him to call and sound so severe. Torn between anger and concern, it was the prior emotion that was the overwhelming one. Within seconds fury had taken over me fully. If he was hoping that I would declare my undying love for him he had another thing coming! This was so not a Romeo and Juliet moment, destined to be together through untold hardships? Fat chance! No that was the last thing I was planning on doing! How dare he think I would be that easy to manipulate!

" . . . There are a few things you need to know, call me back!"

My shaking hands were not able to function properly and I very nearly sent my coffee flying over Lucy, as if things were not strained between us enough as it was. Spilt tea over the quite nice peach pussy bow fitted blouse she wore would not have gone down very well. This wasn't fair!

Sunday 19th June
Barbara Streisand and the Star van

The day is finally here, I have been using the holiday as a mind block from the voicemail. I have even made the decision to leave the mobile at home in case the thought to call him back crossed my mind over the next few weeks. No it wasn't going to happen!
Seraphina and I are now an hour into our journey even though it's still obscenely early. The knock on the door at half past four this morning woke up the rest of the family, a very sleepy Mrs Singh opened the door front door to my always perky friend. Seraphina demanded I got up immediately. The first thing remembered was sitting up on the side of my warm bed. She gave me a few minutes before grabbing my shoulders and shaking me out of my sleepy bliss. She refused to give up until I was fully awake. She had said to be ready first thing and that we would be better setting off as early as possible, but half past four was ridiculous!
"Come on you!"
She bounced on the bed like the most annoying child. It was ok for Miss Perky with her long crumpled gypsy skirt and looks to faint for! Her tight top that highlighted her best assets and the dangling coin chained belt that hung from her waist. I'm sure she got that from Istanbul last year. The long dangling earrings with feathers on them finished off the whole look.
She obviously had festival style down to a fine art.
Knowing my friend she would have woken up thrown on anything she could find and would still look perfect. I on the

other hand had to spend weeks pondering the same outfit. This had completely slipped my mind like so many things did.
That morning I had gone for the flowery wellies, an old baggy sweatshirt (that hid a multitude of chocolate cake related sins) and my favourite deceptively named skinny jeans that went with absolutely anything. I wouldn't need to be 'festival' until I got there. This felt like a bit like cheating as I wasn't totally in the spirit of things, but it was half past four in the morning.
"You look nice"
She looked at me and was disappointed with my choice of dress, I wanted to reassure her but there wasn't time. We were like the odd couple, she had the bohemian chic and I was spotty and in what could have been lounge wear. I hated being awake so early! The bags had been packed; my fake Louis Vuitton holdall and matching trolley case came with me as I stepped out waving goodbye to a blurry eyed Mrs Singh. It was still very difficult to look my land lady in the eye after I had found my hot pants in her laundry basket.
The two of us stood before the genuine split screen Campervan with a very bad blue and green paint job. Granddaddy of motoring himself! Yes they have a cult following and I loved them even more because the hunk next door owned one. Perhaps deep down I hoped for something more along the lines of a Chelsea tractor. A vehicle more equipped to negotiate the rough terrain we would be driving through. Never having been to that part of Europe before I imagined it to be mountainous, there was no way we would get there in a creaky old motor. The paint, obviously cheap emulsion would soon begin to peel and chip away and reveal the original paintwork. This will be a blessing in disguise; anything had to be better than the blue and green splashes across its surface. Perhaps I shouldn't have been so hard on it at first glance. I felt sorry for it.
"Great isn't it?"
Wishing that I had as much enthusiasm, a meek smile was my response to her. Cold feet were seriously beginning to set in at that point. It was far too late to even contemplating turning back now even though I had to fight the overwhelming need to run and hide back under my bed.

"Right get your stuff in we're going!"
The inside of the Campervan was 'interesting'; the old stiff door creaked open to reveal it. A prelude for what was to come. It definitely looked bigger inside than the exterior promised.
The furnishings had not been changed possibly since the sixties. Plush but worn velvet floor cushions scattered concealed what I guessed was a floor in need of a good refurbishment. Although they did look inviting, there was something inviting about the tactility of them. They were just so big and huggable! Next there were the pair of retro printed curtains on one of the windows, in a very retro mustard and brown pattern. They would have made a nice A-line skirt! Nevertheless they were our curtains and would give us a little more privacy when on the road. Not that anyone would want to peek into this clapped out old banger of an iconic vehicle. It was nice to have a little bit of extra security though.
"Where? How did you get it?"
There was the distinct smell of incense sticks, coconut juice as well as of teen rebellion. I realised that this sort of road trip should have been done many years ago. Still it was better late than never for my coming-of-age adventure.
"From a commune I was at last week! We have it on loan for two months. See! I told you everything would be all right in the end!"
Trust Seraphina to find us a 'Magic' van for our adventure into the unknown!
Making myself comfortable in the passenger seat I saw more of the van. There was a mountain of value pack crisps in the corner and several large packets of what looked like continental bread sticks. This was great and would keep us going for a while.
"The pound shop in town is great! We have got loads of goodies!"
I spied from the corner of one eye a portable fridge. This was a start and our adventure instantly began to show promise once again. At least ten cans or bottled beers could be chilled in this thing, depending on how long the battery would last. To my complete surprise there was an old record player in another corner. One that really was as old as the van itself, I hadn't seen

one of these in absolutely years. The last time must have been at Aunty Edith's house when I was a child (mother's cousin who she didn't like to talk about very often—who always seemed rather nice to me) that was way back in the eighties!

This was really fantastic we were going on a sixties style road trip and going to be real life genuine hippies. Ok I didn't quite have all the clothes but hey that didn't matter—this really was hitting the road with love and peace. We have everything we need!

"Oh yeah I forgot to tell you, there's only a Barbara Streisand LP"

Barbara Streisand was with us in vinyl form; she would serenade us with her album called 'Love Songs'.

"Just came with the van"

This seemed unlikely but we would see, maybe if we were lucky a good conditioned Engelbert Humperdinck record or if we were very lucky a Des O Conner album from 1968?

She shrugged.

"It was free!"

That was something so I wasn't going to complain. This year neither of us could afford an all-expenses paid luxury holiday. It was a case of tightening our belts and having some semblance of a break or nothing at all. I looked at my severely over enthusiastic friend, how did she even feel awake enough to smile? I didn't know but it was infectious and I fed off her inner joy.

Looking around at the grey skies I couldn't imagine what possessed me to pack a few squeezy bottles of high factor sun cream. Fully aware that we are not yet in mainland Europe the weather couldn't be that different from home. Norway was not Istanbul and the chances of getting any sun would be pretty slim. The pale skin I had from the long winter months could really do with even a thin layer of tan.

"It's called Star! The guys that have let us borrow it named it that"

My beautiful friend was a complete crackpot and it was times like this that it was so obvious.

"My turn first then?"

I have told her on numerous occasions that I only had a Provisional driver's license but I have the sneaking suspicion that she hopes I will take over for a few hours. Until she realises such a time I have been made chief map reader and have the piles of road maps somewhere in my luggage. They are the really huge fold out ones that show every single road route everywhere in Europe. I have decided not to bother tackling the luggage just yet, not until we get to France and that's a few hours away still.

We are currently making our way out of London and towards the south of the country. It is serene with the beginnings of the day's traffic starting to appear. Seated now next to Seraphina; she's used to me writing and is currently watching the road like a hawk. It makes a pleasant change to be together in practical silence, instead of our usual incessant chatter about frivolous things. This doesn't really happen too often so it's now about making the most of it while it lasts.

The world is coming to life through the hazy morning dew, minute by minute it's waking up. As it yawns and stretches I have a thought, and it's this: After today things, in fact life as we knew it would never be the same ever again.

* * *

So it's about eighteen hours later and we have travelled most of the journey to the South of England, the M20 was plain sailing at that time in the morning which was a true God send to say the least! I couldn't have coped with dealing with traffic as well as trying to wake up—and I wasn't even driving! Ha!

The silence at the beginning of the trip hadn't lasted as long as I had hoped. The inevitable happened and we got talking, as one does on a driving holiday with one's best friend. She started off with telling me about herself, this served as an ice-breaker. I know that she was seeing a guy some time ago. Very nice and well to do, he had young devil children from a previous marriage that he was very mysterious about.

The spawn included a twelve year old boy and a seven year old daughter. They were apparently demonic in nature and would do everything in their power to make Seraphina's life a misery. The gentleman in question was quite particular about his hair which my friend thought was quite 'namby pamby'. It was dyed jet black on schedule every two weeks, this hid the greying sides and made them non-existent. Without fail he would be on time at the salon, his hair covered in cling film-like wrap waiting for the deep colour to develop. She was expected to wait there with him as this happened. In fact she had to be with him everywhere he went and listen to his 'nonsense' as she called it.

He would talk about everything and how he was amazingly brilliant at everything he did. At any given opportunity he would be more than happy to demonstrate his intelligence on every subject known to mankind. I asked her why she was with him for six whole months. Forgive me for stating the obvious but that's half a year and a long time to be seeing the most annoying man in the universe! And having to put up with his spawn as well, they obviously didn't like her so the feelings of pure hatred were reciprocated.

She managed to dodge the question and went on to tell me that she found the sight of him with a plastic covered head repulsive. She had to tell him eventually needless to say he wasn't too happy about this. He offered to take her out and wine and dine her. This is where I got the impression that this could have been a reason why she stayed with him for so long. She sometimes surprised me and this was such an occasion, here was my friend who was all about saving the planet, being eco-friendly yet she loved the jewels and the dresses. So it seemed to be a case of what could she put up with for the wonderfully expensive gifts. Would I have done the same thing? It would depend on how repulsive the man was (that's an awful think to admit to I know)

Perhaps that's why we are such good friends? Because we both seem to hold diamanté encrusted jewellery in fairly high regard. I instantly questioned my own choice of man; yes like Elizabeth Taylor I also was severely attracted to men with lots of, shall we say 'funding'. Perhaps this was why it always seemed to go so wrong?

Anyway soon reciprocation of gory details was demanded of me.

"So what's going on with your Nev?"

The question came as expected. It was a sign of trust that I disclose my love life-related woes to her. It was my turn to talk about Neville and how the relationship really wasn't working out because he has been in hiding since last year. I didn't want to face it just yet, not with things still being so raw.

"He disappeared off the face of the earth until yesterday; he left me a voicemail and wants me to call him"

She gave me her daytime chat show expression, incredulously wide eyed and angry. Seraphina was ready to pounce!

"Oh you are not seriously going to call him are you?"

I shrugged

"No I'm not!"

"What did he want? Did he say why he wants to speak to you?"

These were the same questions that had flown around my own mind since listening to the voice mail yesterday.

"He said he needed to speak to me but didn't say about what"

Seraphina looked thoughtful for a moment as once again the same thoughts flew through her mind as they did mine.

"Right so he didn't give you a clue, a hint as to what it was about?"

My stomach churned at the thoughts, my mystically dressed friend had put on her psychoanalysts head, and that always spelt trouble with a capital 'T' when she did this.

Her sharp eyes looked forwards as she clutched tighter onto the steering wheel.

"Ophelia . . . Is he?"

" . . . Having an affair?"

Finishing off her sentences generally came easy for me and even more in this case as I had been thinking the same thing. As painful as it was I had to admit that she was right. After all if she could see it then it had to be glaringly obvious to anyone.

" . . . It has been a while since you have last heard anything from him; I know it's hard to admit darling but it will be better for you in the long run to just confront the issue now"
The lump began to rise in my throat as I did the absolute best I could to push it back to the murky depths from whence it came. Seraphina was not one to be bogged down by things like 'men', her free spirit was enviable! Now it was crystal clear why she and so many other women didn't let their emotions get too deep, it was just so much easier that way!
"You don't need the drama! Always thought you were too beautiful for him . . ."
There was a short pause in which she smiled reassuringly.
" . . . Besides we have all those lovely great big Norwegian blokes to look forwards to meeting!"
I loved how she had her priorities straight! As lovely as it was that my friend did her best to console me it didn't feel like it was working. I wasn't sure that I wanted to be pursued by a rabble of rather large men being ultra-friendly towards me. One or two maybe but not as many as Seraphina was suggesting. On the other hand perhaps this would take my mind off 'him' making it a little bit easier to move on. Maybe a nice man at the Sankthansaften would be the perfect 'rebound guy' for me!
The tiny and speeding thought crossed my mind, if only I had my phone with me! I should have at least brought his number with me! Why had I not memorized it? Closure would have been something and the ball was in my court so to speak.
Even a: 'Sorry Ophelia there's someone else and we are now engaged!' or
'Sorry Ophelia I'm having an affair with a man at the office!'
. . . Even worse still!
'I'm already married . . . Several times in fact and am a serial bigamist'
Total love rat more like! However maybe he wasn't doing any of the above. The answer could have been as simple as something like he had been in a coma for weeks. And that he had only just woken up and recalled our whirl wind romance from last year! Could he have had an accident and then a leg needed to be

amputated because the gangrene had spread too far for his limb to be saved?

That was no excuse he could still pick up the phone and called earlier. I would have rushed to his side and been his willing servant! I desperately wanted to believe that there was an innocent reason but let's face it, there wasn't!

He was obviously seeing someone else! Most likely a high flyer, I pictured her to be young extremely pretty with large eyes. Her eyelashes would set off a hurricane with every blink! Tiny waist no bigger than the girth of a pencil, long shoulder length flyaway chestnut hair with pert boobs. Jealousy took hold at the thought and I shuffled deeper into the seat.

Moi . . . Jealous, never! This was an emotion I wholeheartedly vowed I would never spare on any man! Seraphina watched me closely from the corner of one purple sparkly mascaraed eye.

"He is a total moron you know! Girl how could you ever be happy with a man who is bound up in a suit and tie all day—He's obviously a 'yes' man to the powers that be! Is that the sort of man who will be faithful to you? The job will always come first!"

He was the sort of guy that my mother prayed day and night for! She would dearly love for me to marry him and would have something else to boast about to the ladies at the Bridge club.

" . . . Trust me all shirt and tie with no personality is not the way to go! You will always be let down in the end!"

Seraphina seemed so adamant about this, knowing full well she had seen her fair share of failed relationships. Perhaps I should take her advice? Maybe her way was the best way? To meet lots of people and go on lots of fun dates! She looked over at me her eyes bright as she caused the sudden revelation that trickled over me.

"You are young! You have plenty of time to settle down; age is just a number anyway!"

I didn't want to hear it; there is a massive part of me that is still madly in love with Neville. So strong was this feeling that I felt that this bond would never be broken! I would be spending the next week slumped beside her in the Star van dying with a broken heart. My downwards spiralling thoughts were too dire for words and Seraphina picked up on the vibes. She ran Indian head massage/psychic workshops back in London so it was second nature.

"Why don't we put on a bit of Barbara?"

She nodded over to the turn table; music was the last thing on my mind as

I still fought back the tears. I hoped she would change her mind and opt for a good old game of 'I Spy' instead but she urged me to do it.

"Go on!"

She quietly nudged me her small frame moved off the cushions for a second.

"... Really?"

"Yeah go on! It's what we need, a good sing-a-long!"

Was she serious? I trundled off in my zombie-like state to the back of the van. After a brief fumble through the wreckage of bags and other paraphernalia, there before me was the only source of music we had.

I saw a corner of it as it was squashed up between on wall of the van and my fake LV holdall. Barbara Streisand, 1981 Love Songs. I looked at the back there were a few favourites, songs that I remembered as a child. Little did I know what listening to the veteran crooner's voice would do to me now? All these years later, 'You don't bring me flowers' and 'A man I loved' and the worst of all was 'The way we were'—sent me straight to blubsville! I was in tears, floods of them. I just didn't need to hear about unrequited love that had been lost. The sheer emotion welled to the surface and burst forth from within like a dam.

"There you go just let it all out, you will be fine! Crying is such a good therapy!"

Her soothing tones helped somewhat as I caught my breath. It didn't feel like the best way to deal with it.

"Maybe this isn't a good idea; I know what it's like when Barbara starts!"

I wish she had thought of that before insisting on listening to her!

Darn you Streisand and your beautifully romantic tones! The diva's crooning had exposed my very raw core. There was some consolation in the form of the cool beers that had been stocked in the fridge, a pleasant and much needed surprise to see the several cans and a couple of bottles stashed in there. Drowning my sorrows was the only way to get through the night. I don't think that Seraphina felt too great about being left out as she was driving. Well seeing as it was me who had the recently failed relationship it was clear that I needed urgent alcoholic attention!

While sipping on the second or third cheap continental beer from the discount store back home I realised we had forgotten one thing-Chocolate. The first chance we get I will find a newsagent's type place and stock up on the sweet stuff. The crisps came in handy though and I could at least feed Seraphina as she was driving. Come morning and I will need my fix! At some point soon a six pack of Aero would come in handy! With all's bubbly goodness it would have helped dispel the inner anguish I felt.

It's now 10pm and we are in the first motel type place we could find in Brugge. I've not been able to see much of mainland Europe so far as it's dark. But it's amazing that we have made it this far in one day so that is something to be pleased about. Seraphina is miles away in the land of nod. It's so wonderfully silent without the constant wittering and attempts at making sense of my failed love life. So lovely that I took the opportunity to have one last semi-warm shower, after tonight there was no telling when the next chance would come. My criminal tendencies almost surfaced as the thought of 'borrowing' the spare toilet roll and bar of soap I found in the bathroom crossed my mind. Luckily it was only fleeting and I managed to shake myself out of it soon enough. Now it's time for some much needed shut eye!

Monday 20th June
Coffee

The Four O clock start at the beginning of our journey proved more than I could take! The first chance I had I let myself go into the deepest slumber on record. After having had the wonderful night's sleep I awoke to a drooling Seraphina by my side. The image was a strangely satisfying one. Her once sparkly purple mascara was now dull and dirty grey in colour. Her mouth was open and the noise that came from the obviously mucus lined nasal cavities was hilarious. I can only describe it as sounding like she was unknowingly blowing raspberries.

So my friend wasn't as flawless it seemed! The make up falling off her skin revealed blotchy skin just like mine. I didn't feel like the proverbial ugly duckling anymore which was wonderful. She snored like a 45-year old brickie (No offence to brickies however my point is that she wasn't always dainty and sprite-like) yes it seemed that even she had what I like to call 'arse-scratching' moments.

Once we had both finally gotten up Seraphina had spent most of the morning in the shower. Once again she had planned for us to be on the roads again for six, but it was soon approaching 11am and we were still both floundering. I'm sure I remember hearing her mutter something about the hotel soap being nice and continental smelling. I'm not sure but I have the sneaking suspicion that I will see that bar of soap again in the not so distant future.

A sweatshirt and a quick brush of my hair later and was soon ready to go. Seraphina took another hour pasting on the make up in a 'Well you never know when you could bump into Mister Right' way. This was a lot of primer, and then foundation in thick layers before the mascara with the eyeliner to give her a smoky eyed effect. I however didn't pack any make up because I thought that this was going to be a 'free-love' hippie sort of thing. No make-up was required where it will be about letting our skin 'breathe'. That's it really wouldn't matter if I look like a big dotty frog because everyone else will too. Feeling a bit cheated by this I considered asking to borrow some, but then again I have also heard about all sorts of strange diseases one could catch by sharing make up. Conjunctivitis would not be a good look!

We were about to set off but not without some proper sustenance. The humongous fry up that was served up gave the impression that the people who run the joint were very accustomed to their British visitors. They had it down to a fine art. Never let it be said that I was a girl who didn't like her food! My breakfast was dripping with fat and that was just what I needed. Rashers of bacon, baked beans and toast, scrambled eggs (I'm particularly fussy about these) everything perfectly done the way I love it! The icing on the cake was the steaming hot cup of coffee that came with the package. Something warm and sweet to wash it all down with, preparing us for the road!

But this was no ordinary beverage that sat in front of me looking all innocent in its large mug. As far as I was concerned it was like the hundreds if not thousands of coffee's I consumed every year. I had absolutely no idea of what I was getting myself into.

The woman who had just served us glowered over in our direction. She was obviously bored with her lot and wanted something to occupy her mind. Aproned and over made up, once she had served us with breakfast she went back to her perch at the small window and watched the pair of us like a hawk.

"Maybe she thinks we are 'together'?"

Seraphina's voice lowered as it always did when she joked.

"Well if we were then we would be amazing!"

Miraculously there didn't seem to be an awkward moment after my last comment! Instead the two of us hardly said anything as we wolfed down our greasy piles of food. But I pondered this more as I watched my friend eat. Surely life would be so much easier if this was the case? Her good looks and my practical mind, we would hardly argue and things would get done! No! I had to stop thinking like this!

She was my best friend and no I just couldn't! I decided to turn my attentions back to my almost finished breakfast, reaching for the coffee cup if I knew then what I knew now things would have been different. I would so have opted for a nice cool glass of water instead!

Taking the handle I lifted the mug to my lips, the heat that the brown liquid threw off could have powered a small country for a week. I took a sip and gulped it down without another thought. Not long after did I sincerely wish that I hadn't done this. Not only was it strong but it was super strength coffee. Is this how they like their beverages here on the mainland? The caffeine shot straight into my blood stream; within seconds I felt the familiar buzz only times a zillion.

"Are you OK Ophelia?"

My worried looking friend had been sipping hers throughout the breakfast; it didn't seem to affect her as much. Her Caffeine tolerance levels were obviously much higher than mine

"I'm fine"

I managed through vibrating teeth. That was this morning it's now afternoon and I'm still on a high, this is scary, hope it wears off soon how long can a girl buzz for?

* * *

We have found ourselves in Frankfurt, Germany. This is miles away from where we should be on our planned route. We or should I say Seraphina took the wrong turning and we are now at least a hundred miles away from our intended destination. It might have had something to do with this coffee-induced state when reading he map out to her. I really should take some of the blame for this mistake. From Dusseldorf we continued to Cologne and not long after that we ended up here in Frankfurt, in completely the wrong direction! We should be somewhere in the North of Denmark nearing the ferry that will take us to Larvik, Norway. Something told me that things wouldn't go to plan! They never did.

So now we are in the middle of Bauer Wurfl Frankfurt, Praurheim. On this gloriously sunny day there are many square miles of Strawberry fields in front of me with hundreds of people picking the delicious looking red fruit. My friend has dashed off not seeming to care that we are nowhere near where we are actually meant to be. She has taken a basket and gone off to join the Strawberry pickers. This will add to our sustenance for the next few days, still this was better than being on turbo strength coffee and calorific fry ups. Maybe a mega blessing in disguise as ever since New Year's I had been threatening to do the whole healthy eating thing. Now there was no longer a choice, it would be strawberries and remnants of the value pack crisps or starve! I will have to just go with it until we hit the nearest burger joint. They were everywhere so it surely won't be long until I could tuck into a quarter-pounder. What a drool worthy thought!

I watched the edge of her long gypsy skirt trail out of sight. I expect her to come back with basket loads of strawberries but I think she maybe a little distracted by our new found friend. Yes you've guessed it she has found herself a new crush. This is slightly annoying as I saw him first! So I am now furiously scribbling this all down on the back of an envelope found in my holdall, my note pad is somewhere in the rubble but this is too precious an event not to recount!

Well about an hour ago we pulled up at the main entrance to the fields, we were meant to sign in and then take a basket. The only place for miles that seemed to have civilisation we had to stop with the intention of asking for directions in my very broken German. But we were there—this was the serendipity of it a road trip.

Ready to pay for our Strawberry picking tickets there was (as expected for this time of year) a bit of a queue and the two of us waited. The back and side doors of the star van were open and basking in the summer sunshine. Somewhere in the UK there had to be a rescue centre for abused Campervans, in the harsh reality of the daylight did I really see how bad the poor thing looked.

I thought about maybe asking Cole to help once we got back, maybe he knew of a good garage that could help. But this was just another excuse to speak to him; I made a mental note of this and added it to the long list of reasons already put together in my mind. Apart from that the beautiful rays of sun were glorious and if we hadn't been lost then this could have been a nice day.

But the fact was that we were totally off the beaten track and in the middle of nowhere with a van. I desperately needed to use the ladies. Holding it in for three hours had not been an easy task and I worried about even attempting to look for one. That itself could have been a dangerous mission as one's bladder was already using its full capacity and then some. I had braced myself for the possibility of actually bursting with the pressure at least two miles back.

" . . . Ello, do you need some help?"

A total revelation appeared to me in the form of the very handsome Christophe. Tall and gorgeous I was in awe and forgot all about my bladder for what felt like a second but was probably ages! How else can one describe male perfection other than the form that this man projected to me? He was beautiful with deep brown chocolate coloured eyes that I could have quite easily swum in. His soft French accent was the equivalent of velvet to my ears. The shoulder length dark chestnut coloured hair flowed in waves around his shoulders, the sun hit it and natural highlights of it shone a fierce auburn. The strong muscular facial features were reminiscent of a modern day Adonis! His upper body was built and muscular, something told me he had done more than Strawberry picking to acquire a body like that! The pristine shirt was unbuttoned at the top so I obviously did my best to get an eyeful.

"Ello?"

He whispered again after my non responsiveness and he studied me, his deep eyes scanning my coffee overloaded form. This man was curious and had wanted to know more, I couldn't believe my luck! What a hunk of a man! It had been absolutely ages since anyone that hot approached me; it was usually me doing the stalking so this was a real breath of fresh air. Quickly I put on my rational head despite being on the verge of a huge swoon.

"I'm fine! I'm just here!"

This was a good point, what could I say to sound blasé and interesting? I was going for a fashionably 'didn't care about anything' look.
"I'm just . . . You know"
He chewed on the tip of the pencil he held in one hand, those eyes again flashed up and locked onto mine. Then the perfect crescent smile arrived on his strong muscular jaw, I don't quite know the words to describe it without sounding corny. He made me melt on the spot, so much so that I was really was about to burst.
"Ou est le toilets please?"
He laughed, again another thing he did perfectly!
"It is just over there!"
He directed me and I nodded thankfully and walked in the direction he aimed at. My gaze however was fixed on him as I craned my neck over to where he stood! Within a split second of our exchange there was Seraphina, talk about bad timing! She waved at me like the most embarrassing aunt would. Anyway remember what I said about her being my absolute best friend in the whole wide world? Well totally scrap that! That day she totally betrayed me!
She saw that I was talking to Christophe the hunk (remember I had most definitely seen him first! By rights she should have left me to it, it's the unwritten rule the man should have been mine!)
So here was the dilemma: To go and tend to the call of nature or to claim what was mine! I had to regrettable see to the prior even thought I would have rather been fending off Seraphina's advances towards Christophe.
Finishing what needed to be done quickly I rushed back to the action. How could I possibly compete against her small perfectly toned body and non-existent waist? I guessed that she would turn on the charm to the fullest, and that's precisely what she did! It was infuriating!
"Hello there! Yes we are travelling through Europe and decided to stop by!"

Christophe smiled that smile again that would make angels cry tears of joy (a little over the top but he was gorgeous!). He was divine and deserved a great big halo!

"This is ze perfect time to come to us . . ."

No kidding it was! I instantly loved the way the corners of his handsome thin lips pulled back causing the dimples to appear just under the apples of his cheeks. His smooth flawless tanned skin no doubt from the days spent out in the continental sun working those abs picking strawberries. Hard and toned I could have run my fingers over the ripples. Maybe on the deck of a yacht on the ocean, just the two of us!

"Oh so are you here a lot then?"

Seraphina jumped in and interrupted my erotic daydream! My mind fell back into reality with a big bump. I had to stop this girl and her whirlwind of seduction in her tracks! I nudged her out of the way.

"Yes tell us!"

"Oui yes I am! I work here over ze summer"

Oh my goodness mega swoon at his totally beautiful accent again! Every word he spoke could have been sugar coated, in my mind I rolled around in the luxury of it all. If anyone was going to take my mind off Neville here was the man to do it. I needed him more than Seraphina surely she should have realised that!

"Wow that's amazing!"

Seraphina was doing the wide eyed 'I'm-really-interested' look which was a big facade to cover up what she truly interested in! And that was getting hold of those abs!

"Yes I help out here for a few months"

Once finished putting my eyeballs back into their relevant sockets I tried hard to smile through clenched jaw as my competition eclipsed me completely.

"So do you, if you would like to have dinner with me . . . I mean us . . . And maybe show us around Frankfurt . . . Only if you are not doing anything that is?"

I had to hand it to her she had guts!

I wondered if he ever got fed up of it, the constant adoration from bored single older women—possibly not as he silently and smoothly agreed to join us for dinner. I HATE Seraphina for destroying my chances of a fantastic affair! But if it's a fight she wants then it's a fight she will get I saw him first! He's mine mine mine!

Tuesday 21ˢᵗ June
More adventures on the star van

Midsummer begins here! It's technically summer solstice, the time when nature balances itself out. Both night time and daylight hours are equal (that's the science part). Maybe one should feel at harmony with everything around them but alas this is severely not the case.

Sitting here in the Campervan, now the middle of the afternoon I'm once again hungry and desperately needing a wee. Fed up of having to synchronise my bladder with everyone else's, and I say 'everyone else's' because there has been a change in our situation. Christophe is now with us and he's is driving!

So you will obviously want an explanation, yes I thought you might: Well last night after a long day of picking Strawberries we ended up staying at a little quaint hostel type place. The baskets of Strawberries stayed in the back of the star van while the three of us took a well-deserved break. (Probably wasn't a good place to put them in hindsight) Of course this would have been so much better had it been just Christophe and I. I pondered the thought of having been on this trip completely alone like Thelma but without Louise. Christophe and I would have gotten on like a house on fire, he was obviously interested enough to come over and speak to me first. It would have been him and I wiling away the hours last night at the restaurant! Instead it was spent mainly watching the two of them canoodling over our candlelit table. It was almost too much to bear for my by then delicate digestive system. The conversation went something like this:

"Wow Christophe you're so great, dedicating your time to Strawberry picking like that!"

"Thank you I love it!"
"I'm sure you do, so you must love Strawberries then? I bet you put Strawberries on everything! (Seraphina giggles)
"Yes I put Strawberries a lot on my cooking!"
"Wow that's so great, it must be why you are so handsome then?" (She giggles again)
"Thank you that's so kind!"
(Christophe bows humbly)
"So what do you do for the rest of the year then? I mean when you are not here in the fields?"
"I paint"
"Ok like houses? You want to come to London and paint my house?"
"Non, I am an Artist!"
"Ah Oui! Bon! Now I understand, you must show me some of your work!"
Listening to all would have made me laugh had it not been for the fact that it was Christophe she was chatting up. So the evening was tinged with a layer of bitter jealous rage, the only remedy was to munch angrily on breadsticks for most of it. I glowered at the two of them but they didn't seem to notice, this infuriated me even more.
Seraphina tried really hard and even spoke French! She had never spoken a word of French in her life and now all of a sudden she was Edith Piaf! But then again anyone would learn another language in a flash when faced with Christophe!
"So maybe you can show us around your lovely town?"
"Well I am travelling through Europe at ze moment"
"Oh really how interesting! So where are you off to once you have finished here?"
"I am travelling to Denmark and then to Sweden"
I felt my eyes roll to the back on my head when she said what she said next:
"We are going in that direction why don't you come with us?"
He looked thoughtful as he sipped his wine and then within moment's . . .
"Yes I will like to come with you"

And that was that settled the two musketeers had now become three.

As mentioned above he is at present driving the star van and chatting quite happily in his sensual French accent to Seraphina. Sitting beside him in the passenger seat she is chatting back in the most flirtatious way possible while my blood is positively boiling!

I have been bundled unceremoniously at the back with the luggage. Basically everything I have so far said to try and get a foothold onto the conversation has been dismissed. Several times did I receive a look that old odd sock gets whenever it was pulled out of the washing machine. There wasn't any point trying to get a word in edgeways.

Christophe is also a free spirit type like Seraphina, they have that in common so I don't stand a chance!

I watched the fields pass us as we drove, they stretched on for miles no one would actually hear our screams if Christophe turned out to be an axe murderer. I shuddered at the thought of this extremely cute guy being anything other than lovely. My attention soon turned back onto the pair in front. Seraphina is still chatting hours later; he obviously switched off at least an hour ago! There was only so much of her constant boasting that even the most handsome of men could take. Either that or he really wasn't the sharpest tool in the box and it didn't matter any way.

Among the topics of conversation have been: How lovely her gene pool is (which is why her long hair that has managed to stay split-end free for years). She has got it into her head that this man is the father of her future spawn. Yes he is handsome but it's not all just about a pretty face as I am quickly coming to realise. If it wasn't for my friend what on earth would we have had to speak about? Perhaps he was the shy quiet type?

I'm not sure how much I like this road-trip idea anymore! It seemed great with the fresh air, the freedom. But now the reality of it all has hit home, I still need the loo and have been sleeve tugging for ages now. There is no sign of a loo break happening any time soon. When one needs to go one needs to go, and that's all there is to say on the matter. There has to be a solid iron clad case each time I need to go. I have even had to threaten to release myself in the star van to be heard!

This worked and we stopped in thirty seconds of me finishing the sentence. However I worry that this threat will get old and will not have the same effect.

Food supplies are running short, I have finished off most of the value pack crisps, there are a few bags left from the forty five there were to begin with. But these bags are the flavours that nobody wants. Beef flavour is hated in the van and so is Prawn Cocktail, these will just have to be the emergency supplies when we really are deserted. This will hopefully be never if we manage to avoid any further short cuts and driving off cliffs.

The beers and other cans have more or less vanished. The Strawberries have gone off quite quickly in the heat of the van. Some of them have been salvageable and I'm picking them apart from the spoiled ones now. It's something to do apart from listening to the flirting. I'm peeling a rancid part off one of the fruits I hope to eat. There is finally light at the end of a long and tedious tunnel!

* * *

We are well on our way to Sankthansaften and now driving through Denmark. This signifies that we are closer to our destination. The next leg of our journey will involve getting a ferry from somewhere called Hirtshals to Larvik on the coast of Norway. It's been absolutely ages since I got onto one of these; the ferry at Woolwich was possibly the last time in about 1988. Not that there is an aversion to ferries or water, London only really has one big river. If one doesn't need to cross it then all well and good, if one has too then there are numerous bridges that can be crossed.

This was the only way to cross onto Norwegian soil; the other option was to drive the long way around. No the ferry was really fine! Christophe parked up in the relevant bay. We got out and walked up some very steep stairs to the sound of seagulls. The very shiny and immaculate passenger area was like something from a glossy travel brochure. These places really existed! Talk about swish!

With gusto and chivalry Christophe pranced over to the cafeteria and ordered coffee, I asked for tea instead. Despite the effects having worn off I wasn't going to risk it, my insides could not take another dose of caffeine ever again!

The first time I had been alone with my so called 'friend' since meeting Christophe I didn't know what to say to her.

"What's wrong with you then?"

I was shocked that she was oblivious to the crime she had committed! I shook my head at her, too tired to bother with beginning an argument with her.

"Nevermind!"

She could have him! That was the most grown up thing I had thought in a long time. Maturity felt good!

The unobtainable Adonis returned with our drinks and made himself comfortable.

"So Ophelia you have not told me about yourself!"

Typical! The moment I lose interest in him he becomes interested!

"Well I am a . . ."

Seraphina sure hadn't given up on him; her designs on him were as strong as ever.

"Oh you don't want to hear about her! I'm far more interesting. I do . . ."

The absolutely shameless self-publicising was almost too much to bear! Christophe seemed to switch off again and looked to the cafeteria he had just come from. But it wasn't just a random gaze; he was looking for something or someone. His eyes rested on a group of people at the cafe ordering their drinks. They must have been there while he was and looked like a university class group about to go hiking or something from the way they were dressed.

One particular girl had caught his eye. She was very small and dressed head to toe in hiking gear you could hardly see her. Early twenties and with the thickest lensed glasses you could ever imagine, the heavy fringe skimmed the top rim of the spectacles. The shy girl looked over in our direction for the briefest of moments and then away again concentrating heavily on her drink that she carried over to the group. I looked back at Christophe and he was totally besotted with her. I knew that look I had seen in a million times before. This was the look that must have inspired Shakespeare when he penned Romeo gave to Juliet.

I too have experienced this very emotion! The true and pure adoration as I first laid eyes upon my treasured Louboutins, it was as if time itself ceased to exist. They had to be mine there was no two ways about it! But that's another story back to this one. It was a look of pure longing and of a severe unrequited love the sort that Shakespeare wrote about. The girl huddled back into the crowd; she disappeared much to Christophe's dismay. His attention was brought back to us with a thud and Seraphina's chattering. She had been totally oblivious to the looks of love that were exchanged between the two young people.

The ferry trip had begun to come to an end and I felt for the two lovers. One quick glance out of the huge ferry windows and I had my first look at Norway in all its glory. Emerald Green and filled to the brim with acres and acres of pine trees. We made our way back to the star van below ready for the next leg of our trip.

Not only have we at last reached Norway after the worst road trip ever but there's more good news! The batteries on the portable record player have run out! We now have a legitimate excuse not to listen to Barbara Streisand ever again! Ha! Things are going to get better from now on.

* * *

This next adventure needs its own 'semi-entry' so here it is ...
I had finally found my notepad buried under a mound of clothes that I won't wear, it's always the case when it comes to packing for holidays. Let's face it the pink sequinned hot pants could look amazing on any model-like mannequin but this was me. I had to face the prospect of wearing something I would look absurd in and it was far too late to do anything

about it. Still it wasn't like there would be anyone I know there. Sincerely hoped not anyway! The thought of seeing Sebastian here sent a shiver down my spine—this wasn't a good shiver. I could imagine him mincing over to me a full speed screeching at the top of his lungs. After the Chantenay Carrot's fiasco the last year Sebastian was the last person I wanted to be in a field alone with! (It's a long story told with full glory in the prequel—you can get it on Amazon!)

The other reason I didn't want to bump into the council loudspeaker was that I knew he would take photographs of my terrible outfits and post them onto all the social networks. Yes every single one of them! By the time I set foot on British soil I would be laughing stock for years, nay decades to come.

I pondered these thoughts as a very desperate Christophe needed to use the little boy's room. There was nothing around so it had to be what we had begun to call a 'field stop'. He had been begging Seraphina to stop the star van for the past three miles, but she was determined to get up to speed. Even if that meant demanding that Christophe reigned in his bladder and 'held it in' for just that little bit longer. I'm sure that to stop your fellow man or woman from going to the toilet was an infringement of human rights!

Finally we stopped and an almost bursting Christophe shot out of the van and into the nearest field. I watched the clouds as they gathered above us hiding the blue skies of the past few days; it was all quite scarily atmospheric. Neither Seraphina nor I banked on what would happen next as we waited for our new driver to relieve himself.

This was the sort of thing that would scare any audience out of their seats in an old Alfred Hitchcock movie. A silhouette appeared at one of the curtain clad windows of the star van, the first to notice it I held my breath in savage anticipation

"Sera!"

I whispered in a hard whisper.

"What?"

She screeched back to me already slightly miffed that she had to stop for Christophe.

"Seraphina there's someone outside the van"

"Of course there is Ophelia! It's called the world and there are lots of people out there!"
She laughed as my eyes were locked onto the still and silent shadow. Short shallow breaths hurt my chest as panic struck me. Fear swept straight through me, eyelids wedged open I couldn't move a muscle as everything was aimed at the window and the still figure. Just the head and shoulders stood what must have been inches from the window, there was a perm! This more than anything sent the beads of sweat dripping over my face. Whoever (or whatever) this person was, they were intent on frightening the living daylights out of me.
"Oh god I see what you mean!"
Ten years later it seemed and my friend had clocked on to what I was saying. The menacing shadow that lurked outside the star van remained painfully still. The blood had completely drained from my friends normally blushing cheeks in terror.
"Don't move!"
She slowly got up from the driver's seat and wriggled her slender form quickly into the back with me, I fastening down the latch with lightening quick reflexes.
"What do you think it wants?"
" . . . Our blood probably, do you think there is more than one?"
The thought of a cloned army of permed weirdo's surrounding us like zombies was insanely terrifying! This is what it meant to be scared to death!
"What are we going to do?"
We held onto each other quivering like jellies.
"Christophe!"
The third Musketeer had been outside taking a leak. How were we to rescue him? Providing he hadn't been captured already and eaten by the herds of zombies out there!
"We have to let him in!"
"No don't worry about him he likes fields! He will be fine out there don't open the doors!"
There was a loud knocking sending both our hearts straight into our throats.

"What do you want? I don't want to die! I'm too young I have so much to live for"

My friend screeched out into the star van, getting behind her I put my one hand over her mouth and the other one held her arm back. She was about to totally freak out and we couldn't afford to go crazy, not at a time like this. I hoped that if we were completely still they would be fooled into thinking no one was here. They would soon go off to look for fresh human meat ad we would be saved, for a while anyway.

"Leave us alone!"

I felt braver still and wanted to confront this beast from the depths.

" . . . Yeah! Leave us alone we mean you no harm!"

The knocking stopped and so did time itself. This was the moment in almost every horror movie just before the creature reveals itself in full horrific view.

"Maybe we should open the door?"

Was she completely insane?

"NO!"

"Let's just do it!"

"I really don't think that's a good idea!"

"Fine let's just stay in here forever! We have no food Ophelia!"

She had a very valid point, we both instantly agreed on this new course of action. Unfastening ourselves from each other, my knuckles were still bloodless with fear. I moved forwards and grabbed the door handle with one trembling hand, with the other I held on tightly to Seraphina.

She in turn also clung to me for dear life. The door slung back to reveal: A small grey haired little old lady in a cornflower blue skirt suit. This was complete with floral blouse, yellow tights and brown flat shoes. I particularly loved the single strand of tinted fake pearls around her neck. This was a well-dressed zombie!

"We were wondering if you could let us borrow a cup of milk."

. . . A cup of milk? That wasn't the sort of thing that zombies asked for; it would normally be blood or live human flesh to gorge on. The little squeaking voice suited the body it came from, but I knew there was more than one. The second nice zombie appeared as if from nowhere.

"Hello we would like to borrow some milk if you have any please"

The second voice chimed as sweetly as the first did. We were confronted with the two identical twins and I mean absolutely identical. They seemed happy and obviously wanted to look like each other! I wondered which of the two made the first move for the other to follow. Or perhaps they just instinctively knew when the other would move or speak. The short ladies watched on their happy chubby cheeked faces expectant for our reply. The enormous grey and hollow eyes were so striking they were hard not to notice.

"We are alone out here and our car has broken down"

Their otherworldly voices chirped like the sparrows we had a lot of in East London (especially at obscene hours of the morning as I stumbled home).

"I'm so sorry but we don't have milk, we are just waiting for our friend who had to use the . . ."

They both smiled in sync.

"Ah yes . . ."

" . . . The little boy's room! Yes we understand!"

Speak of the devil and Christophe had returned. Relief wasn't the word as he stepped back around to us outside the star van.

"Ah you ave made some friends!"

He smiled chivalrously in the way he did.

"Yes Hello there . . ."

. . . Said one, before the other spoke.

"We are Ceres and Cornelia Creepie!"

The other finished off the sentence. Christophe lifted one hand in a sort of 'live long and prosper' way but without the split fingers, the inner geek had visibly begun to emerge from the hunk!

Did he not think they were weird? Two women possibly in their mid-sixties in identical Jackie-O style skirt suits and pearls! That would have aroused more than mere suspicion back in London. But then on second thoughts that would really have depended on what part of the city one was in at the time. No one would have batted an eyelid in trendy Brick Lane or Camden being full of arty types. The Goths would have found them interesting I'm sure.

There was three of us and only two of them; they were outnumbered so in case they turned into violent versions of the Stepford Wives we would be prepared. I quickly thought of an escape plan. Seraphina and I would jump into the van while Christophe fended them off. We would be eternally grateful to him for sacrificing his life for ours. We would drive off as fast as we could and roughly guessing would probably have a good couple of miles head start. That was before the two grannies polished him off and came after us. It was all figured out but then Seraphina did something awful! Devastating in fact!

"We have nowhere to go; yes our car has broken down"

They whispered pitifully, their voices sounded like a sad song. Glancing over at the absolute wreck of a car, it was a tin can on wheels quite literally. But then that was rich coming from someone who was travelling through Europe in a badly decorated Campervan!

"We don't have any milk I'm afraid, but the next services is only a few miles down the road we can give you both a lift?"

The expression on her face told me that yes she was indeed serious about letting them into our van. Was I the only one who could see the potential murderous tendencies that these two ladies clearly had?

"Yes . . ."

" . . . We would like to come along with you"

They fished out their luggage from the unsalvageable car. Three worn out holdalls and a giant suitcase later and the three of us were in the back of the van. Seraphina and Christophe sat in the front leaving me with our new guests. I had to position myself so that my limbs could accommodate the extra luggage. The compact little ladies seemed to be comfortable enough perched on top of the big suitcase. But the silence that soon grew was awkward as I was left to entertain the ladies.

"So where were you both heading?"

I subtly scowled at the sight of my friend pretending to hold the map when she was actually gawking at Christophe. He let out a string of what sounded like curse words in French at the large herd of cows that had decided to cross the small country road. This didn't seem to bother his number one fan; she would always be in awe of him whatever he said.

"We are on our way to the festival . . ."

" . . . The festival that marks the beginning of summer, the Sankthansaften?"

Great! Too spooky to be true but then nothing surprised me anymore. So their actual surname is 'Creepie', they finish each other's sentences and wear the same outfits. The icing on the big weirdness cake was that they were going to the same place we were. The fates were truly having fun with this; I sincerely hoped they were all enjoying it!

Seraphina replenished Christophe with food and drink as he drove, proving to him that she would be perfect 'wife' material. She nudged me from the front seat.

"Ophelia please could you pass Christophe and I a packet of cheese and onion crisps"

Ha! More like 'Pass his royal highness of handsomeness a packet of the finest cheese and onion baked potato chips now!'

She was still on her romantic rampage to our hunky companion's heart. I begrudgingly rummaged amongst the empty food packaging looking for the right flavour, flattening it with my palms as I did!

I had one of my sneaking suspicions that I had finished it off half an hour ago, every last delicious crumb. There was nothing as I searched every nook and cranny for even a small sample sized packet of biscuits (I'm sure Seraphina sneaked a packet into her handbag from the motel at Brugges) We didn't even have a small stamp sized packet of salt let alone a full packet of crisps. It was official we were totally out of resources!

I pulled myself together out of the mild panic. This was Europe and not the middle of deepest coldest Antarctica-there were shops here! Although we had left it to the absolute last minute to think about replenishing stock we were coming up to a small town type place. The neon lights flickered as they had begun

to switch themselves off. The sun had begun to rise, we had literally travelld through the night! I prayed that the sign was a supermarket and not a bingo hall, luckily my instincts were spot on and it was and I celebrated inside!
" . . . Stop the van! We need food!"
"Shall we come in with you?"
"Yes we can help!"
Perhaps it was judgemental but I shuddered at the thought of going anywhere with the Creepies. However not wanting to seem rude I nodded, surprising myself. It was interesting the lengths a person would go to in order to seem polite, I thought on this as we pulled up quickly into the deserted car park. Christophe needed another pee break badly unlike Seraphina who seemed to have the insides of a camel. Although a very handsome guy he had absolutely no control over his bladder! The two of them were total extremes when it came to their toilet habits. He was the first to shoot out of the Campervan and into the pristine shop. We still had another five hours or so to go until we got to Tromso, that's a long time when it comes to 'holding it in'. Thank goodness for twenty-four hour store opening!
Seraphina waved me off in an 'I'm alright' sort of way so I left her to it not knowing the carnage that would confront me on arrival. How much trouble could she possibly get into? At least I was doing her a favour and stopping them from taking her soul and transforming her into one of their clones, although I didn't see Seraphina ever being happy wearing floral blouses or skirt suits. Picking up a plastic basket from the pile I was ready to shop! One of the unwritten laws of food shopping says that one should never shop on an empty stomach—it makes people buy more. I didn't have a choice, I was starving we all were!
Crisps, fizzy drinks, I found a small bag of a cheese assortment, yes that was definitely going in the basket! Chocolate cake yes! We all needed chocolate cake, it wasn't a luxury. Not bringing the mobile phone was a bad idea. But bringing the credit card instead of cutting it in half after purchasing the Geisha wedges was a great idea! Fed up of counting every single crisp I was by then totally ready to gorge on junk, the aisles of food was a

feast for my eyes. This was my holiday and if I wanted to spend it piling on the pounds then by George that's what I was going to do.

The gateau was dropped in the basket without a second of thought, along with the cans of beer. All the descriptions were in Norwegian so I just went by the pictures on the packages; a Swiss roll was a Swiss roll no matter whatever country it's in. Finally it was time to hit the checkout with all the sugar laden goodies! The gum chewing girl at the till looked at me as if I was a slug, a big juicy one that's slimy and eats fields of lettuce every day.

She put everything through the till slowly and with real meaning. 'Bleep bleep bleep' the familiar sounds were so wonderful I could have cried with joy. Normally in London I would have been embarrassed about buying two large chocolate gateau's as well as litre bottles of soft drinks, what I guessed were five economy packs of crisps in a variety of flavours. The only criteria anything needed to fit were that it was edible and tasted nice. I watched the young assistant with her beaded wrists push through everything with a beep.

"This will be one hundred and twenty euros"

She must have heard me wittering to myself in English as I shopped.

"How much?"

My eyes almost catapulted out of their sockets.

" . . . One-hundred and twenty euros!"

Her voice was stern and she meant business, one outstretched palm demanded immediate payment. She could not be serious! Surely my purchases couldn't have amounted to that much! I glanced over the mountain of food once again; yeah ok there was a lot of it. Would making her feel sorry for me help matters? It had to be worth a try! I wanted to arouse the feelings of pity from deep within her.

However fluttering my eyelashes at her and being as sorrowful looking as possible didn't work, she shot an angry glance at me.

"That is one-hundred and twenty euros, PLEASE!"

Could I have put something away that would have brought the total price down? Maybe one of the chocolate lovelies or six packs of beer? We didn't need beer, on second thoughts we did. Well I certainly did anyway! I scrounged around in my purse for my credit card.

We needed all this junk, what the heck you can't take it with you when you go! I decided to pay up for the goods. It would be more than enough to feed the growing brood at the back of the Star van. Feeling like the Good Samaritan I handed over my fantastic plastic and began to bag up the goodies.

All the while fantasizing about that first glorious bit into a large chunk of chocolate cake! From the picture on the package it was chocolate on the top, in the middle and at the bottom as well! Mega yums!

" . . . This is not work!"

I looked up at her very bored gaze.

"Sorry what was that?"

She stopped chewing,

"This card it's not working"

Panic flew through me like a lightning bolt. I had fallen at the last hurdle, so close but yet so very far off!

"What do you mean 'not working'? It always works!"

"No it's not . . . Look at this!"

She swiped the credit card through again and the till display indeed flashed 'cancelled' in bright luminescent red, so bright that the whole world could see! My mind whirred in a state of confusion, was I currently being done for fraud in the UK and didn't know about it? I needed money fast and there was no way I was going to leave the store without food.

Back to the van and a lot of grovelling was called for, something I loathed doing.

"What do you mean it doesn't work are you a criminal or something?"

Christophe threw over a shifty look; clear he wondered if coming along was a good idea.

"Look Seraphina I'm hungry and we still have another few hours to go—Its one-hundred and twenty euros! Pay up please!"

She groaned and fumbled through her bag and pockets for loose change. I put all of my thirty euros to the campervan collection, having had spent most of my cash on the last tank of petrol. The Creepie twins were the next to empty their pockets, between them about twenty-five euros. Seraphina coughed up another twenty-five and Christophe came out with the remaining wonga needed. The girl happily received her money and even helped me with the bags as I left; she did so with an unmistakable expression of glee.

That was earlier and now I am writing to you from a field somewhere in Norway. The gang and I are having an impromptu picnic. Bright azure skies cover us; there is not a cloud in sight. I absolutely love that smell of warm summer afternoons, its musky and sweet at the same time.

The fields before us stretch for as far as the eye can see, like a patchwork blanket. It's really beautiful out here.

Wednesday 22nd June
Body hair

We are here in Tromso at last. That's all well and good but I've not had a wash since that night at the Motel. One physically feels too disgusting for words! But this is the sort of thing that is on the card when one signs up for road trips. And how the topic of body hair had slipped my mind is bewildering. Every self-respecting woman of the world should always tackle this subject, especially when going on holiday! But it really had completely slipped my mind, possibly because of 'that' message! I had intended on bringing a set of disposable 'lady' razors with me, but alas it was never to be. The thought of having to dry shave with one of Christophe's razors in the back of the Campervan is not appealing at all. Any feminine charm that I did have would disintegrate in a second. No! One needed a private bathroom with purposely pink razors and wax strips for that sort of thing. There was no choice but to sit tight and wait until I got home. The only realistic option is to borrow one of Seraphina's floaty skirts and hide the growing leg hair; there is nothing I can do about the Frida Kahlo look although bushy eyebrows seem to have been all over the catwalk this season. Fashion has given over plucking big thumbs down! John Galliano seems to have spawned a movement against over plucking. This is all well and good it's just that I haven't had a mono-brow since I was twelve.

That glorious day when I picked up the shiny precision tweezers and first placed it to my jungle brows, instant popularity ensued. Invited to be part of the 'in' crowd, I was soon a user of mascara and eye liner—a staple part of my make-up kit ever since. Right now while I'm here in a big field full of hippies there is nothing I can do to stop things from taking its course when it comes to hair. It really is 'Just as nature intended' is the fashion statement to go by for the next week.

I simply cannot believe that now at about half past one in the morning Seraphina has left us to make some new friends! Christophe is asleep; he zonked out the moment the Campervan was parked in its bay. We are now alongside the many other newly arrived and also zonked out drivers. To our left is a couple in a car far away in the lad of nod, one of them is drooling (yes I can see it from here!). I wish I had brought my camera this was all great material for some entertaining social networking site photo albums

* * *

Five hours sleep later and I awoke finding myself in the back of the van. For the briefest of moments before waking one was at home in her own bed. Never before have I appreciated so much the double bed in my room. The way I can do starfish impressions on it! I can fling my arms around and not accidently hit one of the creepies sleeping on the floor! Yes my bed at home is fabulous!

A good night's sleep would have been enough to ensure the under eye bags were not too noticeable.

However they were awful this morning! I peering into the small compact mirror I keep with me and there they were. Something

would need to be done about these when I got home. Whatever a week's worth of sleep wouldn't cure-Botox had to!
I took my first glance of Tromso in the daylight, it was big! Covered with hundreds if not thousands of tents and caravan's, I even spotted a few large motor homes in the distance. Compared to our little star van they were mansions on wheels! I looked on in jealousy; I bet they even have bathrooms in them, an awesome big one where the inhabitants were able to have place to wash and 'tidy up'.
Continuing to scan everything from the small window, the whole scene before us was bizarre to say the least. Like some kind of warped circus with a big top. At the centre of it all was the semi completed bonfire, festival goers of all ages were still adding to it, with twigs and old planks of wood (one wondered where these came from—and hoped they weren't plank napped from someone's hut!). Traditionally these huge bonfires were meant to be seen along the edge of Norway and the rest of Scandinavia so they have to be massive! One couldn't help but love the air of expectation and freedom that this scene revealed.
Costumes of all kinds were worn-I spotted a native Navajo Indian head dress on one party goer along with leopard print onesie. As expected fashion-wise this was a world away from East London.
It's been hours and there's still no sign of my friend who was acting like a stray cat. It was at the exact moment we arrived when she spread her festival wings and flew off into the sea of mysticism.
Well that was all well and good for her, but some of us liked our beauty sleep!
An age later I managed to crawl out of the van and was instantly greeted with the scent of frying bacon. There are few things in life that are more wonderful than tucking into a well cooked bacon sandwich. The Creepie twins had somehow acquired several rashers of bacon that were quite happily sizzling away in a frying pan on a stove. I'm sure I hadn't seen these in the van, they were either very well prepared or had 'borrowed' them from fellow happy campers. The loaves of bread bought

yesterday had come in handy also being toasted on the frying pan. This was all great and I wasn't complaining but there seemed to be burger stalls everywhere, they could have saved themselves the hard work!

Christophe was also nowhere to be seen, I imagined he was out there looking for somewhere to wash and have a shave. Seraphina would be in tow once she had had finished surveying the festival. I had to admit to myself she had won him over. Bitter and betrayed? Not anymore I was over him and men in general. The first bite of the Creepie made bacon sandwich seemed to signify a new Ophelia!

This was good bacon butty; they knew exactly how much ketchup and salad I liked in my sandwich! It was perfection and made me feel instantly better about things. I looked up with a huge mouthful as I munched, both the twins grinned at my contented expression.

"We hope you like your breakfast . . ."

"Yes we really do . . ."

Nodding as I bit off another big chunk of the sandwich, which was too beautiful for words. Maybe I was really very wrong about the twins? They weren't too bad after all. They were quite nice and I appreciated their efforts. Unless it was all a façade! And they had put a spell on the sandwich? They had bewitched my bacon! And now I too was also under their spell and would before long become one of their minions! But that was fine, as long as they would cook for me like this I'd be happy to go along with their plans of mass devastation. In fact one could capitalize on this! Spells for sale could include a 'Leave your friend's potential boyfriend alone' spell! Or a 'Find a better paid job' spell?

I had a moment when my thoughts became words.

"What have you done to the bacon?"

"What do you mean Ophelia?"

How rude I sounded, accusing them like that! Quickly a 'U' turn was needed.

"I mean do you have a special ingredient because this Bacon is fantastic!"

The ladies looked at each other and smiled, baring their identical sets of teeth. I shuddered as subtly as possible.
"Does this mean you like the breakfast we made you?"
I nodded furiously
"I loved it!"
Hands clasped together each of the ladies semi bowed to me, and smiled even harder.
"That makes us so pleased"
Chimed one
" . . . Yes it does"
Did the Creepies turned Seraphina into something weird like a llama? (I always thought if she was ever an animal she would be a Llama and I would be a Husky) Maybe Christophe was one as well? Maybe they were both Alpaca's that the Creepies would take back to their lair and use them for producing wool? That was a horrible thought, the two of them as long necked sheep like creatures kept for all eternity with many other unfortunate victims. And then maybe I would buy an Alpaca sweater or other product and feel a particular fondness for it. Something within would tell me that this was wool from my two friends that had disappeared long ago at a festival in Norway.
Why could I not switch my brain off from thinking these hideous thoughts? This was irrationality in its highest form, it had to stop.
I finished off the rest of my glorious sandwich; sweeping up the last drops of sauce with a piece of bread. This was the epitome of being full and happy as I sat back on one of the floor cushions in a contented heap. I absolutely loved the Creepie twins and really couldn't care less if my sandwich had indeed been cursed.
"Coffee?"
"No it's really fine thank you"
My decision on that was pretty self-explanatory, so I won't go into that. Instead I thanked my new best friends and went back into the van to don the most outrageous thing I owned. Yes you've guessed it my sequinned hot pants! One simply had to join in with the celebrations after travelling all that way. I excitedly pulled them out of the trolley; they were as pristine

as they could possibly be! I swelled all over in pride—but not just pride. It came to light that the swelling was also a result of breakfast. They didn't fit!

I took another deep breath and tried again. It didn't work no matter how desperate I was to get the top button to fasten. Wanting to mingle with the rest of the festival going folk I needed to step out and be outrageous.

Ok one more go I breathed in and was soon practically shrink wrapped. Using all my strength I willed the button to hook into place, it worked! Some celestial being out there thought it right for this to happen and I was thankful to them. Even though the button hole was at its full capacity, clearly it would stretch no more, the button lay half fastened and half undone. I just needed it to hold for the day! Cautiously I let that painful breath out wanting to ensure that I would be safe to move around without bursting through my over tight hot pants. One could have screamed and leapt for joy but decided against it for fear of jeopardising things.

The downside was that this had left me with the most disgusting muffin top on the planet. But hey! It didn't matter because I finally had them on! Even though every breath would be guarded, and one would have to be careful when smiling or talking (eating was totally out of the question!)

The heat of the summer's day meant I could wear my vest top and expose most of my body, which was great! Springing forth like the excited little lamb that one was, the Sankthansaften was my oyster!

I did indeed mingle with the crowds and met more than a few very interesting types.

There was so much activity going on with much of it centred on the main bonfire that had gotten a lot bigger. It was almost there with the finishing touches being done to it, I noticed a strange kind of structure that had been built above it. A wooden stage with what could have been a noose at the end of it. Was there going to be a public execution? I dreaded the thought, surely not in this day and age. I dismissed the thought as quickly as it had entered my mind.

Apart from that the place really was buzzing: I hadn't seen people that excited since the last Topshop sale began. There really was an infectious mood which grew every minute and I loved it!

Everybody I passed said 'hello' or 'hi', there was no way this would ever happen in London. But here it was accepted and I also enjoyed smiling like a loon. If anything this trip was beginning to become one of self-discovery.

Not only had I 'discovered' that I could now fit into the hot pants but also that I now had hardly thought of Neville at all. This was great and just what was needed. Maybe all that mumbo jumbo about things happening at the right time was true? Maybe we were all meant to come here to take part in these midsummers' proceedings?

All was well with the world at that moment; the rest of the day was spent mingling with the other festival goers who had also travelled in from all over.

Despite my differences with her I was so glad Seraphina had talked me into coming along on this bizarre road trip. Despite all the trials and tribulations we had made it and it was awesome, tomorrow will be even more so! I don't know how I'm going to get any sleep tonight; no one else looks like they will be sleeping either. Lamps have now been lit and folk music turned up to full volume. As tempting as it is to join them, refraining and sleeping is now on the agenda, apologies for being a little on the boring side but I need as much of it as I can get after today!

Thursday 23rd June
Sankthansaften

This day has got to be one of the most glorious days in living history. Who would have thought that the sunshine could be this strong so far up in Europe? The sunscreen has come in hand after all! I slapped it all on, so I had maximum coverage to sun worship safely.

The euphoric feeling that has been picked up by everyone here is infectious. I'm turning into a great big hippy myself and I truly love it! I don't have the ultra-long hair and long flowing Seraphina-style skirts but 'hippiness' is more a state of mind than what one wears. Hippies say things like 'fingers up to the world we are going to do it our way!' They say 'We are not going to get regular jobs we are going to live off the land and fresh air!' and 'we will not be dictated to by the bureaucrats! We will knit our own jumpers and not use soap and we will be satisfied!'

I am really considering becoming a fully-fledged hippy. This would be a fabulous reason to hand in my notice at work! But would I have to do a University course to become a qualified one? Or take a hippie pledge and promise to live by the 'rules' for the rest of my far out days? More research would have to be done into this.

The crowds of people here have gotten bigger overnight, doubling in size and are way crazier! I thought yesterday's Navajo Indian was strange, I have just seen Abraham Lincoln walk by! The circus really has come into town for the big day with several tents erected. Guys on stilts have appeared as if from nowhere and are walking around lording it over the rest of the midsummer mayhem.

My fantastic day started a few hours ago with scrounging for something to wear on my feet as my prized floral wellingtons seem to have disappeared. The last I remember seeing them was yesterday evening when I had taken them off. Unless they have walked away all by themselves I have the sneaking suspicion that my darling friend Seraphina has borrowed them. She is probably somewhere canoodling with her new beau. Half a shoe size smaller than me, which will not stop her from putting her twinkling toes into my floral wellies!

Back to more pressing concerns and I needed shoes. As if the great fates came to my rescue miraculously I found a pair of flip flops outside star van. The down side was that they were very grotty, like someone had worn them and not taken them off for possibly three years? Ah well everything else was muddy or grubby so it can't make too much of a difference.

The flip flops were a size to big but perhaps this was a blessing in disguise for when squelching through acres of mud. I hadn't had to do that yet thank goodness but it didn't hurt to be prepared. One thing I was pleased about was that I had bothered to do my toenails. My toes were just as sparkly as my friends!

There was a strange scent on the air mingled in with the hot dogs and the grass, it was unlike anything I had ever encountered before or hopefully would again. It had to be one thing only, the combined scent of thousands of unwashed bodies frolicking in mud on Sankthansaften. I say that as if people are somehow smellier on the 23rd of June than on any other day. There may be some truth in that as it is technically meant to be one of the warmest days of the year, it follows that people will smell worse.

After a while one became immune to the 'at first' nauseating scent. Soon things were as fresh as the freshest mountain air! For a girl who follows fashion, one who often flicks through fashion magazines-this experience was liberating. At one with nature I chose to wear my own personal 'natural scent' with pride. My lengthening leg fuzz growing with every passing second was smiled upon by a midsummer's sun. Once home Sebastian would pick up on the 'cave woman' look, that would be my reputation ruined so it made sense to make the most of it now.

After finding some shoes I began to make very long lengths of daisy chains, random? Yes very! But the result was very beautiful as we didn't only use the traditional 'Daisy' but all sorts of flowers and plants. The resulting chain and smaller flowered crowns looked more like richly decorated garlands than the simple chain that one would make as a child. The ladies who sat around in a large circle varied greatly in appearance. Tall, short, young and mature all were joined together by this chain of flowers.

Sitting on the only dry patch of grass that wasn't covered by motor homes or tents we produced lengths of these chains. A weird sort of flower coven there was a link between us women. The strong feeling of sisterhood and female bonding with the goddess was overwhelming I really loved it! How great it must be to be truly at one with nature!

There had to be some mystical reason as to why we were doing this? Or maybe there wasn't? The one thing that was clear was that the ladies in the group were deliriously happy. Surely that was reason enough to be there in the midst of their weird flower related joy.

Anyway the big Christophe news is this, well remember the shy girl in the group on the ferry to Larvik? The one who wore those big thick lenses and was all covered up in hiking gear? Yes I knew you would, she was unforgettable in her own special way. She is here, it turns out that they were making their way to the festival too. Of all the festivals in the entire world she came along to our one, even though it wasn't technically 'our' festival but you know what I mean.

In his own awkward but special 'Christophe' way he managed to strike up a conversation with the hard-to-crack anorak yesterday. Apparently he sidled up to her and said 'hello'; yes it was really that simple. With those good looks and conversational skills he got through to her within seconds according to a 'none-to-pleased' Seraphina. These two were obviously meant to be together right from the first longing gaze across the ferry cafeteria!

A glorious shiver went down my spine; things really did have a way of working themselves out in the end. My faith in love has been instantly renewed by this romantic tale. She recounted all this with a pinch of salt; she had lost him to the beautiful anorak! I secretly gloated inside as I put on a sympathetic face to her, now she knew how I had felt and we could go back to being friends again. She smiled at me for the first time since we had left home, filled with a warm fuzzy feeling I knew things between us were back to normal—But I have learnt a valuable lesson from this. Never must we let a man get in between our friendship ever again!

I spied the happy couple over by hiking camp; the briefest of smiles went over the cute girls face as Christophe chatted with her. He actually looked shy himself! There must have been something about oversized weatherproof coats that did it for him? They were still chatting by midday, there was some serious romancing going on over there. Minus the heavy duty specs she could actually be quite a stunner. I watched the scene unfold from the van and caught the flash of that handsome smile, she grinned back cheekily.

It was love at first sight as I polished off a burger that the Creepies had made. Magic or not I loved anything they cooked! I pondered for a moment if I could take the twins home with me? I knew that my land lady would find a place for them to stay, once she had tasted their wondrous magical cooking. Now she was someone who appreciated a good meal.

This festival way of life was brilliant! I could see myself going from day to day not worrying about things like future mortgages or loans for the future shoes I will possibly (most likely) be buying. Everything here was borrowed from the flip flops on my feet to the clothes I was wearing. One of the Creepie sister's pushed a plate of fried eggs on a toast into my hands interrupting my thoughts. Was there really enough room for more food? It took all of two seconds to think about it concluding with a resounding 'Yes!'

"They make a nice couple don't they . . ."

" . . . Yes sister they make a good couple, yes they do!"

The mysterious voices of the two lingered over to me as I ate and nodded while filling up my face. They had by now won me round, no longer were they the soul-sucking harpies that children had nightmares about, I liked them and their burgers and eggs!

Now that Seraphina and I were no longer vying for the attentions of Christophe, she had invited me to meet her by the 'psychic tent'. This wasn't a tent that knew exactly what you were doing before you began to do it. No the tent in itself was not psychic. It was in fact a big green tent in the middle of the field that housed a group of crazies.

These nutters claimed to know things about your future; I pictured old women asking me to cross their palms with silver. It would be all crystal balls, tea leaves and all that mumbo jumbo. She had said something about wanting me to meet someone that would change my life forever. A strange look passed over her face as she spoke, the mysterious shadow that had no explanation. All this happened just before she dashed off to join the rest of them in the tent.

Curiosity and intrigue were aroused by the tank load and once I had finished breakfast I wobbled my way to the giant monstrosity on the landscape. The huge green tent was almost as big as the bonfire had become, you could not miss either of them. I loved walking over in the grubby flip flops and the gypsy style skirt that must have 10 metres long (One that I borrowed from Seraphina seeing as she also 'borrowed' my floral Wellington's, it was only fair!)

The crowds in the big construction were teaming in the heat; it was filled to the brim with very flustered and warm festival goers.

"... Ophelia!"

She screamed the way my mother used to do, when summoning me from the other end of the supermarket. The big wave from my friend signalled her whereabouts as she jumped up from the crowds. I pushed my way into the throbbing crowds accidentally running into a cling-on who growled at me. Once I did get to her I found my friend clad head to toe in a bright and unmistakable forest green. This had to be one of her special planned outfits for today. We eyeballed each other

"Isn't that my ski ... ?"

"Oh I so glad I found you Sera! You look great! I love the green!"

"Thank you yes forest green symbolises and encourages fertility and growth!"

It certainly seemed to be the colour to be wearing at midsummers! As if my eyes were from that moment programmed to be drawn to the green, there were a few folk in the shade of forest green. One thing for sure was that it soon started to encourage a headache.

"Anyway are you sure that ... Isn't that my ... ?"

Yes I was wearing her long luscious gypsy skirt! One of her loveliest one's. I could deceive her no longer and decided to come clean.

"... This skirt? I found it, in the back hope you don't mind!"

I had indeed pulled it out of the mass luggage in the back of the van. The mound that was made up from all our belongings and had soon amalgamated into one. I spied the edge of it from the corner of my eye, the light earthy colour of the crinkled wrap skirt I had seen her wear before. But yes I did know that it was hers and chose to overlook that.

" . . . Never mind about that!"

She waved my desperate attempt at redemption.

" . . . There's someone I want you to meet"

If it wasn't Christophe's twin brother I didn't really want to know. She could see the blasé expression on my face as I desperately wished that he had a single twin brother.

"I think this could be very important for you Ophelia! She asked me to bring you to her"

Was I about to be fed to the mother beast? I had a feeling that would happen, or sacrificed to a strange midsummer's cult. Images flashed through my mind of being fastened to a massive corn doll and sacrificed to the lords of the harvest. The people of the tent and indeed the rest of the festival goers would watch on as I met my demise, they would laugh and dance in glee to the sound of pan pipes. All very horrific like a badly seventies horror movie! Inwardly shuddering I awoke from these imaginings and faced my over enthusiastic friend.

"Come on!"

She grabbed me by the hand and led me worryingly deeper into the heaving crowds. Don't ask me how or why but at that moment I sensed that a major event was about to occur.

* * *

I was led to the most remote part of the tent; the small corner was cordoned off and was surprisingly quiet. In this small velvet curtained room was seated behind a floral topped fold-away table the most jewelled woman ever. Yes cocktail rings are really in at the moment and so are bangles but this was ridiculous. It was a wonder that she could move at all, but she dealt those tarot cards with the speed of light. The jewelled psychic could have been a poker player while she wasn't doing her day job.

The next thing one noticed was the half-filled bottle of Tequila and two shot glasses that were not used; here was a woman who obviously didn't like washing up and wasting time doing it! She was a 'straight from the bottle' sort of gal! It had taken my eyes a few moments to acclimatise to the major bling that she wore. The lady herself was someone who had seen life, small and wrinkled she resembled a ninety-something year old prune (if there were such things in existence). The coins that dangled from the headscarf that wore over her forehead tinkled gently as she moved her hands and head dramatically.

No crazy celebrity costume in a wacky music video had anything on this woman as I surveyed her costume in detail. There were a lot of glass beads in the intricate tunic style top she wore. How could I ask her where she bought it? But she looked like she was concentrating on something far deeper than fashion. There was no way she would have heard me anyway. I saw the heavy wrinkles scrunch up in her face and move into a bitter expression as she motioned for me to sit down. Like she had seen my whole life in a split second, things didn't look good or so I thought.

I made myself comfortable as my host began to wave her hands palms hovered over the cards faced down on the table. There was a low growl as I looked over to Seraphina for moral support.

The lady picked up the bottle of Tequila and took a swig before sighing in satisfaction; this was the fuel that powered her mystical powers. She mumbled something that resembled words but in another language, of course this couldn't have been easy with no teeth. Holding my breath I could vaguely make out what she was saying.

"I see you have brought your friend here, as I asked of you"

"Yes and here is your payment Madam!"

Seraphina stepped forward bravely and placed a pound in the palm of her one awaiting hand.

She nodded in acknowledgement of payment and quickly pocketed it before turning back to me.

The old woman stared at me through grey and aged eyes, the immense gaze held me.

She saw something in the future that I didn't, was she going to tell me when I needed to schedule my first Botox session? I hoped so because I wanted to be more than prepared for the onset of aging.

She grabbed my hand and pulled it along with the rest of my arm sharply over the table. Her appearance was so deceiving! Looking so weak and feeble yet sending me flying closer towards her, I had almost sent the Tequila and glasses flying. My friend had long since disappeared, what a time to just go like that? I could forgive her this any other time but not then, this wasn't fair!

"Young woman I have an important thing to tell you!"

Her face was full of concern as her bony hard hand held mine tightly, so tightly that my blood supply to it had completely stopped.

" . . . You are to face a difficult decision, one that could change your life; you will make the right one so trust in yourself and your instincts!"

Yes I knew it! I should book that Botox session as soon as I get home, the choice was clearly take preventative measures now or wait till things got worse. She took another swig of her Tequila and pushed me away back to my seat. Straightening up the cards she waved over them again and groaned in a low deep tone.

"I will read for you your cards now"

Furiously flicking them over one by one, these cards were not the ones that are seen in the movies,. One card had ancient symbols that resembled something that I wanted tattooed on my wrist a year ago. This was when I went through my 'Cheryl Cole' phase as I like to call it. She surveyed each of the symbols and then closed her eyes before looking back up at me. We were eye to eye now and a bizarre thing occurred. It was as if our souls had merged for a short time, I could have known this woman all my life, the sense of familiarity was so incredibly strong.

"I see that there will be a time of confusion, I see this happening for you. There is a sense of loss in your personal life"
The indescribable spine tingling moment to top all spine tingling moments happened.
"You must follow your heart; there is no other way as it will lead you towards the right path, the only path!"
She looked at me waiting for some form of reassurance.
" . . . Promise me that you will do this!"
I nodded at her vigorously as she again grabbed onto my hand tightly. Right then my instincts were telling me to get hold of a stiff drink. I was thinking an ice cold double vodka and coke. What did she mean by 'difficult decision? And following my heart?'
It was clear that this was about more than delaying the ageing process with Botox!

* * *

The experience I had just been through had shaken me up; this condition wasn't helped by my friend deserting me. I mean she drags me over there and then disappears like that! I pondered on what the lady had said but these fears for my future were dispelled almost instantly when I spied the candy floss cart. This always did it for me, there was nothing like the pink fluffy stuff to put things into perspective. I tucked into the glorious pink delicacy after managing to scrape together some of the pennies I had left from the shopping trip.
The scent of burning filled my lungs; the smaller bonfires across the field had already been lit
To cheers from all around.
My eyes had almost become accustomed to all the weird and wonderful things to see out in the open but I soon found my eyes being drawn to a small child. Dressed in an oversized green raincoat and multi-coloured beanie hat, the child sat on a floral printed deckchair which was far too big for the tiny frame. Next to him was a cardboard box, the contents looked like they could have been laundry, but on closer inspection I

found them to be the most colourful jumpers imaginable. The thick ultra-layered ones that Artic explorers would wear!

This child needed rescuing and I was the person to do it. My steely reserve enabled me to walk over to the small figure. He simply needed to be taken home to his worried parents! They were no doubt at home wondering what terrible fate had befallen their child. There had to be some authority here that would help this poor thing forced to obscenely colourful clothes in the middle of nowhere.

I approached him with caution, in my most maternal way (this was probably a mistake as I subconsciously became my own mother for a few moments).

Soon it was that things were not as they first seemed, this small child was actually a fully formed man complete with fashionable stubble. Yes there was definitely stubble on his chin, cheeks and neck. Totally in total shock at my big mistake, how could I have gotten it so wrong? My eyes stared in horror and awe at the same time. I soon realised that staring was very rude; trying to be tactful I took an instant interest in the contents of his cardboard box.

"Wow those are great!"

Speaking to him like he was a child only seemed to add insult to injury. He grunted back at me, perhaps he didn't understand English? It was very ignorant of me to assume that everyone did. Perhaps he was Norwegian and hadn't understood that I came in peace and didn't want to take his jumpers away from him?

"I-said-I-like-your-jumpers!"

The little man now glared at me in the most evil way ever, in a way even more evil than Amanda sometimes had looked at me.

"Yes I heard you the first time deary!"

With the most high pitched cut glass British accent I had ever heard, he replied back sharply. Talk about the voice not matching the image, when not selling sweaters he would have easily gotten the part of a James Bond villain.

Too shocked to stifle a giggled I felt the need to make amends or some kind of jumper-related karma would come and make my life a misery.

"So can I have a look at your jumpers?"

He turned his mouth up suspiciously, this came with narrowed eyes.

"Why?"

He squinted even harder at me.

"Well because they are très jolie, and I would love to have a look if you wouldn't mind so much"

I would reduce myself to an over excited customer to make this little man feel better. However something I didn't expect to happen did. The more I glanced at the jumpers the more the need to feel them took over. They really were the most intricately knitted of creations and looked so touchable. The same delirious craze descended over me as it did when whenever there was a sale or special offer on at my favourite store. I had to have one.

"Yes but they are not for sale"

He was totally at ease with this controversial comment; he had no doubt said it a thousand times already that morning. The floral deckchair, the big cardboard box full of colourful jumpers, these were all trademark signs of a market trader selling his wares.

"So why are you here?"

Perhaps blurting out my thoughts so spontaneously wasn't the best of ideas; needless to say it wasn't received as warmly as I had hoped.

Note to self: From henceforth keep thoughts in head until they have been fully vetted. Do not, I repeat do not under any circumstances release them without fully assessing each one first!

So anyway back to the very displeased small man:

"I am here because the trolls asked me to display their work here at the festival"

I desperately hoped that 'the trolls' was a clothing company of some kind, or even a band that knitted in their spare time perhaps. That would have been acceptable, strange but acceptable. But to suggest that these beautiful textile creations were the work of actual mythical creatures was just plain wrong! There was nothing for it but to go along with this strange man's fantasy despite wanting to laugh out loud.

"Oh that's nice, do they have a website? Do they sell online or do you have to visit them at their gallery?"

He scoffed incredulously and held back what would have been no doubt demonic laughter.

"No they do not have an online outlet; they live in caves . . ."

This was getting weirder by the second but I loved this guy and his weird world! I wanted to (and still do) take him back to London with me and hire him out for parties, hen dos or other girl's nights out. Or even just to put him on stage with a microphone all he would have to do was be himself. He would win fame overnight online, and I would deal with the 'fortune' part of things. I wouldn't have to ever work again with the revenue that he would bring in, a superb business plan and I was fully hoping to make it happen. All I would have to do was to pick him up and put him under one arm! Obviously I would need to ask him first and then there was customs but we could do it: www.hirelittleman.com would be a raging success!

" . . . You may only look, you cannot buy!"

He climbed back up onto his chair crossed his arms and stuck out his bottom lip rebelliously. The deep creases in the child-like little man's head deepened.

I picked up and held up the sweater on the top of the box. It was beautiful and thick; these designs were clearly made for extreme cold and proved that you could still be jazzy and warm! A year of snow and blizzards could not penetrate this sweater. The colours and the patterns were adorable: A cerise and grey number that could be worn as a sweater dress or in a tunic style with some equally funky leggings or tights. This would be a fantastic addition to my winter wardrobe! Heck I loved it so much I would wear it in the summer if I could bear it despite the blue and pink reindeer everywhere.

This had taken my fancy more than the rest of the gaudy knitwear—but gaudy knitwear is really in! Geek chic is very cool! I loved it enough to offer a price and my adoration of this particular item seemed to please him immensely.

"You know they are one off and made from magic, the Icelandic name for them is 'Lopi'!"

I liked the whole mysticism aspect of it; this was a fantastic selling point.

"So if I was to offer to take this one off your hands how much would I be parting with?"

... In my most convincing bartering voice.

"I told you they are NOT for sale!"

I could see that this wasn't going to be easy but the longer one looked at the jumper the more intense was the need to have one became. It would be well worth the humiliation and fight to get it. But all this wasn't the point! He had no right to bring beautiful jumpers that were obviously made with troll magic to a place like this and 'not' sell them. It was against the nature of shopping itself! Or perhaps this was a strange kind of reverse psychology that he used along with the unique selling points? I obviously had no clue about how trolls did business but I was falling for it hook, line and sinker.

"Hold on I will see what I can do for you"

He whipped out his mobile; he obviously had his bosses on speed dial as in a flash he was speaking to them in either trollish or Norwegian.

I waited and twiddled my thumbs, straining to hear the gruff loud voice on the other end of the phone. Waiting to go into that all important job interview was a lot more preferable to this! The little man nodded a few times in acknowledgement of what he was being told by troll headquarters. Once he had finally finished he sighed and looked up at me with still narrowed beady eyes.

"Yes we can let you have it at a price..."

My pulse raced in anticipation!

"Great! And that price would be...?"

He whipped out a notepad from his pocket and scribbled on it with a blunt pencil before pointing it at my Lopi.

"We can let you have that one for two hundred and fifty euros"

"What!"

"This is the best price I can offer you as each is handmade from special wool!"

'Special wool' He had to be kidding me! It would have had to be made from pure gold for that price. It was in my hands and felt divine, soft and one could really see why it was so expensive but I couldn't give up. I needed this lovely Lopi for my collection. If I left without it then that would have been one of the greatest tragedies of all time. I did not know where trolls lived and didn't fancy the idea of a Nordic adventure to their caves next summer just to try and nab one. It really was now or never! I mean what would happen if someone else got it? The thought was unbearable, simply put this couldn't be allowed to happen under any circumstances!

"So you couldn't do me a special price?"

He turned his nose up at my fluttering eyelashes, instead he looked at me as if I was something that he had found on the bottom of his shoe, but I expected that this man to be a knitwear snob!

"No"

Was the simple reply?

"Two hundred and fifty euros is a lot and we are in a recession"

I grabbed onto my Lopi tighter, the inner spoilt child did not want to let this beautiful thing go ever!

"Not the trolls! They are not in a recession!"

This was all well and good for the lucky trolls but the rest of us were, they really should have counted themselves lucky that anyone could afford their handy work. One of the reasons that I made the decision to do this road trip was that it was hopefully going to be a cheap holiday. This was proving to not be the case with the amount we had spent on food and petrol never mind the added extras (pretty jumpers).

"Well that's even more of a reason for you to give me a deal on the Lopi isn't it?"

He stroked the stubble on his chin thoughtfully perhaps my desperate plea had somehow gotten through to him. The little man was back on the phone again within seconds chatting to

troll HQ, and again I waited and quietly surveyed his raincoat type jacket, he must have had to make a lot of 'cave visits'!
"Ok we can let you have it for one hundred and fifty, that's it! That is our final offer"
This was still a lot but this new offer was less than half price. How could I resist this? Talk about sale of the century, it would be foolish to walk away now. The small man made to grab my Lopi from me; I took one look before my stomach lurched terribly.
"No that's the best that we can do"
The little man growled and watched me and the ferocity in his eyes grew, I didn't want to risk incurring the wrath of him or the trolls! There would likely be a lot of them and they would be angry.
"Do you take Visa?"
The transformation from enraged to calm was instantaneous, symbolised by the warm understanding smile he cordially gave me. Finally we were on the same wavelength! This was going to be my new woolly crush for years to come, I mentally promised myself to never take it off ever! I loved it and was extremely proud of my choice but also with the fact that I had with cunning and grace managed to purchase it at less than half its original price. One was very pleased!

* * *

Leaving the big green tent on a high was immediately confronted with the commotion. The fires had been lit and tension had heightened. The last of the wood was thrown onto the main bonfire it was gigantic as promised. There was no way that this bonfire was going to be missed. I had to crane my neck as far back as possible to see the crackling tips light up the darkening skies.
The giant wooden construction that hung over the bonfire now supported a crudely made dummy. It resembled a witch, dressed in black with pointed hat. Made from straw and cloth the poor thing looked troubled up there as the crowds cheered; she was positively traumatised at the thought of her soon to

be public execution. I watched her and tried to imagine what it could have been like if she really was alive and part of a real life sacrificial ceremony. The fear and terror that she must have felt, I sympathised with this straw dolly hanging up there.

"It's a dummy Ophelia!"

My friend had somehow resurfaced no longer dressed in the forest green of earlier.

"Why did you disappear like that? And why are they burning her?"

She looked bewildered

"What are you talking about? I haven't seen you all day! And it's not 'her' it's an 'it'"

" . . . In the tent earlier? You know with the crazy old lady?"

My friend smiled at me sympathetically.

"Ophelia I think it's you who are the crazy lady!"

I sincerely hoped that she hadn't been taking any odd substances. I stared into her eyes at her pupils, and no they were not dilated.

"You mean you don't remember anything?"

"Ophelia are you feeling alright?"

Despite being a warm evening it felt surprisingly nippy all of a sudden. Who was the woman in green? She had felt real as she dragged me to the . . . I didn't want to think about it.

"Yeah I'm ok"

I was totally freaked out about this in reality! My attention turned back to the witch dummy. One couldn't help but feel sorry for the poor thing all on 'its' own hanging there. The only thing it had to look forwards to would be being burned to a cinder!

"It's just what they do here!"

But it wasn't that easy to watch. I felt as if I could relate to her in some strange way, after all we were both single and tormented she by the flames and me by my mind. She did look lonely up there and could have done with a companion, another lady and loyal friend perhaps, someone to be tortured with her. What if these two dummies were of Seraphina and me? There was no way they would burn my effigy wearing the floral wellies right?

Seconds later as the bonfire itself was set alight she herself had gone up in flames within seconds.

What could this poor thing have done? Most likely something along the lines of being a witch would have done it. Well the only consolation was that she had gone to a better place. One in which she could be happy and run around free in golden fields chasing dogs and people. How fabulous it all sounded but not enough to make me want to be a straw witch myself! Standing there among the cheering crowds I was glad to be human.

Symbolic in a purely egotistical way but it was as if the dummy being burnt was the old Ophelia and a new one would arise from her ashes. One that would be so much stronger than the old! She would not turn to jelly at the sight of a good looking man! Nor would she flounder at the mere sound of Neville's voice no matter how deep and silky it was. No way! This new Ophelia will be strong when it comes to dealing with men but also in regards to dealing with cakes and pastries. I will say 'No!' and soon regain the svelte body that once was my seventeen year old self.

Seraphina woke me up from my thoughts with a new daisy chain crown for my unwashed head. You truly can't get more 'summer festival' than that! I feel like a real seasonal princess as I sit here watching the bonfire light up the evening skies of midsummer. The Creepies have made some friends today and brought this new group to the star van.

I was given a plate of what looked like gruel. One of the Creepie twins told me that this was a delicacy at Sankthansaften! Handed to me by a teenager with cute dimples I had to accept of face his proud parent's wrath, I accepted gratefully. Taking a spoonful of the gooey stuff it was kind of a sour creamy porridge with Cinnamon and sugar sprinkled over the top. I loved the sickly sweet taste that took me back to the days I would add extra sugar on my Ready Brek as soon as my mother's back was turned, those truly were glorious days! The air smelt strongly of ham, barbequed food like sausages and hot dogs even more so than earlier. With drink flowing everywhere people made

merry, dancing and singing. Feeling like I was in the middle of some sort of BBC middle ages costume drama was fantastic!
The party would go on for as long as everyone could stay awake, I too was going to try and stay up until at least three and make the most of every moment. Here I was celebrating summer with the people that had become my surrogate family. I cared for them, yes a crazy thing to say about Christophe and his girlfriend, the twins and the group of other random types but yes I think loved them! There was a real sense of humanity and kindness here that one could never find in any big city, the scary part was that I am stone cold sober as I write that!
One of the Creepie twins was alone on the very rare occasion that she was apart from her sister (she was in the portable ladies loo)
"Did you know that tonight if you put flowers under your pillow you will see the man that you truly love? It's old folklore!"
I looked at her smiling back at me deliriously. How any two people could be that happy all of the time was beyond me but I was starting to like the infectiousness of her happy weirdness. I smiled back and decided that I would find me some flowers to put under the pile of soft clothes that had become my pillow (I don't know whose clothes these were by the way). I simply had to find out who my true love was going to be now that I was practically single and Neville-less! Would he be tall, rich, blonde or brunette? Would our children be supermodels and geniuses at College? Would he have a name like Chip? Or Stud?
It's now the evening and I'm sitting here at the back of the van guarding my Lopi with my life, it's rolled up between the small of my back and the seat. There's no way anyone is getting to it! Ha! Especially not now since I noticed Seraphina sweeping one quick longing gaze over it. She got to Christophe she sure wasn't getting to my Lopi, no one was! So now I am alone here while most of the team have gone to join the festivities. I however have more pressing issues to deal with right now. The Creepies are still here and are snoozing outside the van preferring the stars on this gloriously warm evening.
They are snoring in sync which is very weird and slightly disturbing (I should be used to that by now!) How they can

sleep with the racket going on I don't know! There are people dancing and chanting something to do with midsummers, it was all too wild for me so I opted out and decided to cheer them on from the side lines instead. Maybe it's not the greatest of idea's to be alone tonight of all nights. I'm thinking of him for the first time since talking about Neville on day one of our trip. Things have been too wacky to stop and ponder on the wreckage that was the relationship with him. And Christophe has been somewhat of a distraction for some of the time.

But as much as I hate to admit it Neville had always been at the back of my mind through everything. He has got me secretly wondering how he been doing, what he's been doing despite urging myself not to.

Knowing deep within my heart that I should really have called him, I mentally kicked myself for not bringing my phone with me instead of privately preparing for the worst. At least the phone call would bring some sort of closure on this thing which would be great. Hearing the cold harsh truth would be the only way to get the release that perhaps we both needed. Was my new found bravery just a masquerade for the hurt I felt? Yes most likely but it's clearly over and there's nothing I can do about it apart from face it head on, pick up the pieces and move on. There was nothing for it but to put on a brave face and call him once I get home.

In the meantime there was still the promise of finding out who my true beloved would be. Luckily I didn't have to traipse through the woods looking for a bunch of fresh flowers to place underneath my pillow; there was already a band of flowers around my head. Picking them off my head I surveyed them for their suitability. They were a little worse for wear, but a flower is a flower and I'm sure even the ones that were drooping would still count for something with the Sankthansaften fairies. Placing them delicately underneath my rolled up Lopi (which I chose to place under my head for added security) I lay my weary head upon it. One last look up at the twinkling bright stars through the open door, my conscious mind drifted off to a place where I hoped to find my true love.

Thursday 23rd June to Friday 24th June
Political rally for the destruction of Bunnies

The villagers huddled around the clearing that I was placed in the middle of. Surrounded by peasants with pitchforks and staffs was not the greatest feeling in the world. To my severe dismay I was tied up on a large wooden column that was practically bolted to the ground, I was high above the crowds and looked down on the thousands of angry faces with their threatening screeches. This was the worst kind of history lesson imaginable! I wasn't in East Ham high street or even Romford for that matter. Looking above the rowdy crowds were acres of open spaces with the odd cow dotted on the landscape, all quite nice really if I hadn't been tied to the stake!

Envying the cows I would have swapped places with them any day! Anything to get out of the fairly bad predicament one was in.

Everyone was out to get me, vying for my blood! I had to get out of there but the pitchfork pointing seemed to get more intense every second that passed.

"Wait! Gentle folk of our town tell me what this woman has done!"

The small man with the big wig had fought his way over to me, struggling and grunting through the jeering. On closer inspection he was a little on the grubby side and smelt bad, I was obviously in a time when soap and water were not as freely available as they were in cheap motels.

He screeched with all his might out into the crowds, the only way he would be heard. It shot out into rabble causing a deafening silence. The pause lasted seconds before another pitchfork wielding man jumped up and shouted in reply:

"She claims to have seen the bunnies!"

What was he talking about? I have said nothing about bunnies to anyone! This was insane!

The volume of the jeering had turned up to full blast as it was aimed towards me; I got it from every angle.

"But she is not aware of what she does! Not in her right mind! Leave her be and pay her no heed brethren!"

The grubby leader stepped even closer, despite his lack of hygiene I felt a fondness towards him and his attempts at saving me from my inevitable fate. But the crowds were having none of it and continued in their quest to have me tortured.

"She only wears one earring! That's the sign of the 'Bunny' seer!"

At that point I could no longer bear it I had to say something about all this nonsense. None of it seemed to make any sense. They needed to know the truth!

"I wear two earrings and I have not seen any bunnies since primary school at the farm!"

It was a little strange how I assumed they knew all about the bunnies at the farm all those years ago. They wouldn't know, there wasn't anyone that was recognisable from school here in the crowds. I doubted they even knew what 'school' was!

There was a gasp and then silence, a long and painful silence that I wished was over.

"There! See she has seen the bunnies! There is your proof!"

Darn those bunnies and their fluffiness, how I wished that I hadn't picked them up and cuddled them. Why did I love their little creaky noises when I held them and fed them salad? I had to admit it that I loved those bunnies and still did wherever they were. The small man in the wig was by then totally convinced of my real and clear guilt, I had just admitted it to them. Little wig man was angry! Ferocious in fact and turned on me instantly.

"Don't you know that bunnies are poisonous to us?"

He waved his big stick at me in the most threatening way a small man could, I looked at him as he soon transformed into someone I recognised. It couldn't be! No surely not! Yes it was the small man in the tent who sold me my beloved Lopi, the woolly hat was replaced with a wig. There were still his same burning eyes that shone fiercely from underneath the big hair. I looked down at him horrified; the rest of the crowds sneered at me, they really did want blood and they wanted it to be mine!

"Please don't kill me"

My pathetic voice whimpered out into the maelstrom of anger and bloodlust. I had felt as helpless as the witch dummy hanging above the bonfire. Then it had hit me, I was the witch that I so sympathised with. They were going to do to me what was done to her, there was no way out!
"I hate bunnies I tell you! I hate them!"
Never before in the history of everything was a person so sorry for being a fan of the fluff! I was sincerely sorry for loving bunnies and promised to never do it again!
"That doesn't matter! The fact is that you broke the law and now you must pay!"
Little man in big wig looked like he was enjoying the power, then several other of the peasants came towards me with sticks alight. I looked below me only to my horror that I was on top of the massive bonfire of Sankthansaften!
"Now try to be practical about this Ophelia . . ."
I muttered to myself the way I always did when I was in big trouble like this. Although this would have to be the worst trouble I had been in. Yes this was pretty bad.
" . . . What to do, what to do?"
This mantra was repeated over and over again, it wasn't as helpful as praying would have been.
The heat turned up quickly as the wood below me as the raging flames roared.
"We are the political rally for the destruction of bunnies!"
How dare they want to hurt the lovely fluffy creatures, so innocent in their cuteness! No I would not let it happen . . .
"You can't do that! What have they done to you?"
The big wigged man sniffed as if I had insulted me.
"They eat us! And so they will come for and devour you!"
What in heaven's name was this man talking about? The flames grew higher and higher totally engulfing me within moments. There was a shocked gasp from the crowds that had been cruelly cheering on my torture. The giant bunny appeared it was massive and very angry. Its large eyes looked directly at me unwavering. There were the usual clicks that bunnies made only amplified by a thousand. This creature didn't resemble anything that I remember from my childhood days.

The Bunny lord was angry, it too wanted my blood. Big with teeth that had the worst case of tartar I had ever seen it approached me.

With a ferocious jolt I almost jumped out of the seat that I slept on, a few more inches and I would have banged my head in the roof of the star van. My head hurt, what was all that about? The giant bunny was too strange for words. There had been nothing in my waking life that could have encouraged that monster to appear in my dreams. Thank goodness that was all not real!

The Creepie twins were still snoring open mouthed and loudly. The clock in the van said it was still only half past four in the morning the birds were chirping almost as loudly as the snoring. The commotion outside hadn't ceased after last night; obviously from die hard party-goers who still wanted to eke out every second of midsummers-good on them I thought!

These strange smelling folk were determined to party for as long as their physical forms would allow them to.

I was sweating, so would you be if all that had happened to you! Forget all the drama and the angry shouting, I didn't even mind that I was tied to a big wooden stake and set alight. No my problem was the fact that saw the little Lopi selling man in my dream! Did this mean that we were destined to be together? I shuddered at the thought and quickly scrambled underneath my Lopi pillow to find the flowers. There were there exactly as I had left them, they were thrown as far away from me as possible (which wasn't far as I throw like a girl). For the next few hours my mind was filled with the dreaded thoughts of being in love with little man, of the children we may spawn. I hoped they would take after me height wise but perhaps after him business dealings. I had to admit he was pretty good with that kind of thing. Yes we would have a little cottage in magic land with other magical creatures as neighbours. It would be all so wonderful and actually come to think of it he wasn't too bad . . .

Friday 24th June
Going home

The new nightmare was actually bumping into little man again! How could I possibly look him in the eye again and hold back my amorous giggles after all that we have been through! At that moment I promised myself the holiest promise ever. No one else could know about this, it was to be kept between the Lopi, flowers and me. Neither of the other two would ever utter a word to anyone else (because they obviously couldn't speak) it made me feel a little safer.

The limp daisy chain that now lay on the floor of the van, a lot like my dying enthusiasm for this road trip did. I needed the comfort of my own bed and the luxury of a shower. Oh how I longed for a really good wash! The novelty of the free living free loving lifestyle had by this point truly worn off. Determined not to waste a moment and after partying for all of last night and this morning, my friend managed to have a personal psychic reading with rocks in the tent. The rock reader found out that she responded well to rose quartz which is always a good thing according to her. She will be attracting a lot more love interest into her life, nothing new there then. I'm sure she would easily manage to seduce a fresh faced younger man soon.

She had also found a prayer circle that she had managed to get herself involved with. She was telling me all about the chants that she had learnt while I managed to switch off over breakfast. Focusing fully on my tinned baked beans was so much easier. While living in a van can be cosy with the right people, it can also be too confined, for example there has been nowhere to hide from Seraphina's incessant chatter. It's driven me a little bit crazy; perhaps it's more to do with having slept on car seats for the best part of the week?

As I did switch off I caught something about Seraphina wanting to go to the wife carrying championships in Sonkajarvi Finland (6-7 July). She had planned on taking the star van with me and the Creepie twins in tow. They discussed all this last night while they tanked up on the local beer and dancing. The beard festival has to be pretty straightforward; it would be who has the longest glossiest beard around perhaps? Or maybe the contestants would be judged on particular talents.

Being able to preserve food for long periods of time in them or even grow a small garden from one. The wife carrying festival was another matter completely. My friend would have to find someone to pose as her husband and be carried over the finishing line. The prize: The wife's weight in beer! An attractive proposition but Seraphina didn't weigh very much. She has loan of the van for a while before it needs to come back at the end of July. Telling her I wanted to go home like now, wasn't easy but I truly was at my wits end. I needed a bath!

The lovely girl who is now besotted with Christophe and very much vice versa now has a name; she is Amy and is from Sweden. Within the space of a day and a half they have made plans to go and meet each other's parents and move in together somewhere near the strawberry fields. How lovely is that? Apparently they just 'knew' way back in the ferry to Larvik that they were destined to be together. So love at first sight really does happen! I am so jealous watching the two of them canoodling at any given opportunity.

Right now at this time of writing we have said goodbye to the daisy chain making ladies, Abraham Lincoln and are now on our way to the airport to drop me off. Like a total diva I demanded that they take me to Oslo airport, where I will be purchasing a ticket and taking the earliest available plane home. Yes I admit that this is the coward's way out but I believe that I have earned my right for a simple life. Is my life ever simple? That's debatable.

The Creepies are with me at the back of the van along with the lovely Amy who cannot stop staring at the object of her desires (who is also staring back at her from the passenger seat beside Seraphina). All together now 'Ahhhh . . . '

Romance wasn't on the cards for me and that was fine! I didn't care I was going home at long last! Out of the muddy clothes and into a long, hot, cleansing shower. I had fantasized about shampoo for the past few days and lathering it all over my scalp. Of shower gel oozing on a sponge ready to be scrubbed all over my festival worn skin. The mud that would have to be peeled off from the bottom of my soles will be disgusting and I am prepared for that. After the past week I was prepared for anything!

Did I regret cutting my holiday short and not following the crew to look at bearded men for a full two days? Or being involved in a wife carrying contest? Well a little but as I have already mentioned I have had my fill of sleeping in the back of a van (even though it was the infamous star van) I will never look at Campervans ever again without a smile and a fondness in my heart—perhaps after a few weeks once I have recovered from this traumatic experience!

How could one forget queen crooner Barbara Streisand filling our first few days of driving? Or finishing the last packet of prawn cocktail crisps and wishing desperately that I hadn't? Yes these were all moments that had possibly aged me but it would be, as my friend had put it at the beginning of the trip: 'a journey of self-discovery' and it was.

Sunday 26th June
Gerard Butt-ler at the airport

I waved goodbye to the gang, it was a bittersweet farewell as they drove off into the distance. I was sad to see the Creepies go especially at a time when I was only really beginning to get to know them. It was clear that they were not flesh eating harpies but instead quite good cooks. Seraphina made clear to me as we left that I was not to contact Neville under any circumstances, (now she was my life coach and she would see me when she got back home with tales of the beard and wife carrying festivals.

"Be strong Ophelia!"

These were last words to me as she blew me a kiss before speeding off into the sunset. I was left with my luggage at the entrance of the airport. Practically running to the tickets desk I was a desperate woman. So glad about making the decision to

fly back to London Stansted that I nearly threw my credit card at the man behind the tickets counter.
"What have you got for London?"
The young man said nothing but smiled, he happily tapped away at his keyboard for a few minutes.
"We have a flight at ten in the evening, but nothing sooner I'm afraid"
He continued to smile and waited for me to reply, this wasn't long
"Yes I want it! Book me on it!"
He looked me up and down and yes you've guessed it, smiled again
"Ok I will do that now"
The trauma was nearly over and this was pleasing.
There was something about the brightly lit airport with its haven of well-lit duty free shops. The cleanliness of every surface hurt my eyes at first, half an hour later my pupils had acclimatised.
First stop was obviously the shops; I rushed over to have a closer look. The myriad of shops enticed and excited me, I felt as though I was already home on the air conditioned shop floor. The handbags were amazing, being there took me back instantly to being at Selfridges in London. I know it wasn't exactly the same thing but it wasn't far off.
The preened assistant watched me from afar and turned her nose up at the stench that came with me. I didn't blame her I would have done the same thing had the tables been turned. I on the other hand had become immune to the smell so it didn't offend me at all, which was just as well. As if my nasal cavities had grown another protective layer to cover all the smelling cells.
There were two assistants and they wittered amongst themselves quite obviously at the odd woman who was now threatening to buy something from them. They were debating on the best method on getting rid of me. I felt sad that they didn't want me in their super hygienic shiny duty free store so I took the hint and left. As I did something truly miraculous happened (typical). Yes I saw the man of my dreams; it was Gerard Butler the super Hollywood hunk! In the distance but

close enough to appreciate the fashionable stubble on chiselled jaw and his beautifully muscular torso, middle and legs. He was truly perfection in human form; the best part was that truly butt-tastic derrière!

It was typical that I happened to look like a bog-dwelling tramp at the time this Hollywood-worthy creature came into my life. I doubted myself and my eyesight.

Surely it was him? Even Gerard Butler had to shop! What's to say that he wasn't here in Norway filming for the next movie? I had to get closer and make sure, as one knew every inch of that gorgeous face it wouldn't be long until I was sure. I followed him as he left the group of people (obviously film producer types) and went over to the newsagents. He would be buying magazines; no doubt most of them will be plastered with pictures of him. I followed him while hiding behind my bag lady disguise, mints! That's what I needed; I grabbed a handful of the green tubes and placed them at the checkout while watching the gorgeous figure shuffle around the magazine shelves.

Something was a little odd however; no one else seemed to notice him no camera crew hanging around just him in his tight fitted white t-shirt and jeans. So fitted was this t-shirt that his muscular outlines were on display for all to see.

He approached the checkout and I held my breath hiding my face behind long greasy locks. Why was I constantly falling for a pretty face? This was a bad habit that I so needed to kick even when it came to famous ones!

I quickly became aware of his body nearing mine at the queue for the checkout. I really had Hollywood's golden boy standing next to me! But even better yet—if he saw past my festival exterior and asked me to join him on the set of his next Hollywood blockbuster! I would quickly be sought after by all the big directors, Steven Spielberg, James Cameron to name but a few. All of them would want me for their leading lady in the next big role. Tales would be told of how I was discovered in an airport just like Kate Moss.

This would give Neville something to think about when I was in all the papers! Ha! I was so excited at this point that I could barely breathe. The lady at the checkout was also having delusions of fame and fortune, it was obvious. She smiled; her neutral pink shimmer lip gloss stained her teeth horrendously. I was defiantly the more fame hungry out of the two of us. Deciding to bite the bullet and introduce myself I turned to my side I looked at him square in the eye:

MAJOR EMBARRASSMENT ALERT: IT WAS NOT GERARD BUTLER . . . I REPEAT IT WAS NOT GEREAD BUTLER!

It was in fact a very old man with an extremely toned bum.
"Hello"
His wrinkled features squashed together as he smiled. His large nose turned downwards shadowing his mouth resembling a haggard garden gnome instead of a human.
I quickly paid for my mints and left with a polite smiled at the man who hardly had any teeth. All my hopes of stardom were dashed in a second. How could I have gotten it so wrong?
It's so time for that optician's appointment once I get back home, I can't risk it happening again. Who knows next time it could be a lot worse-Johnny Depp or even Hugh Jackman!
I sighed with relief and contentment as I slumped into my plane seat. This was the best feeling I had experienced in a long time, regardless of that strange smell of the plane and the seat I was sitting in. There were also a few strange looks no doubt because of the dank greasy locks, but it didn't matter anymore. I might as well have been in a cave for the past ten years, but I didn't care I was around real civilization once again!
The flight was about two hours but it felt like longer as every minute could have been a year. By this point I was so desperate to get home but reflected on the past few days away from everything I had ever known. Traffic, the city, pubs and clubs, fine dining and long hot showers!
But I realised that despite my constant whining, (I averaged a 'moan' every second mile of the entire journey there) the whole experience wasn't so bad. I had learnt to make
This is the reflective part where it's all looked through with rose tinted lenses. No there needed to be a hint of realism here. I

didn't like all the mud, and sleeping in a caravan but never mind about all that now. I am homeward bound!

Monday 27th June
Back to civilisation

Hot shower and my bed! Enough said!

Wednesday 6th July
Making 'the call'

So now that I have been home almost a week and after a lot of faffing about I have finally decided to make the call.
I wasn't sure how things would go but I had to do it after making up my mind in Norway. There was no point going over the same arguments for and against doing it, I just had to do it. Heart pounding like a drummer at a heavy metal concert I dialled the number.
The conversation went a little something like this:
"Hi Neville?"
" . . . Ophelia hello! So glad you called I was beginning to think you were not interested"
That voice! The same husky tones from all those months ago lingered to my ears, absorbing into my very core. If it were possible to wrap the sound around me like the softest of blankets then it would have been done. I had to face facts despite trying to constantly talk myself out of my feelings for him I still loved him like a crazy person just loves to be crazy.
"Well I have been busy doing a bit of travelling"
I read somewhere that being 'mysterious' was a trait that men were attracted to, so I didn't give too much away. Heck I wanted him to know that I was getting on with my life,

expanding my knowledge so on and so forth and not curled up in an embryonic position crying over him every day!

"That's great; I have been busy too with work and things"

Voice strained as if he was trying to be just as mysterious, this sounded highly dubious but perhaps I was reading too much into it? I seized the opportunity to change the subject feeling sick to my stomach with big nerves.

"Yes so how is work these days? I imagine it's keeping you busy!"

Again a long pause . . .

"Yes work has been keeping me on my toes as always"

Was he being deliberately vague? He was normally on the ball with things related to work. In the past I have had to listen to blow by blow accounts of minute business transactions. I was beginning to see where Seraphina was coming from in regards to potential partners. Men in suits may not be the best way to go.

"Hey that's great news I know how much hard work you are putting into the business"

Trying to be extra chirpy wasn't coming easy to me. Then he began preparations to drop the ultimate bombshell!

"Ophelia I really need to speak to you about something . . ."

He's had an affair! I knew it! My heart flew into my throat. A great looking guy like Neville would have women throwing themselves at him; of course they would! Even though he was a total love cheat!

" . . . I really should meet you in person to discuss all this! It's not really the sort of thing I want to discuss over the phone"

This was getting more serious by the second

"That's fine, how about tonight?"

There was a long pause, had I sounded too desperate? Yes because I was!

"I'm not able to do tonight I'm afraid"

That's right he would probably be with his lady friend no doubt! The one he has unashamedly picked over me!

" . . . How about Friday night? If you are not doing anything that is . . ."

It took me all of two seconds to give him my answer

"Yes that would be fine, ok I would like that"
Would I seriously 'like that'? After all this time it would be extremely difficult not to mention mega awkward! The last time we were together in person was on an actual date in town.

I should have just demanded that he tell me over the phone, it would have been quick and painless. The added bonus of a phone break-up was that I wouldn't have to face him when he tells me I'm dumped. I pictured the situation as one of his board meetings, seated handsomely behind a large Oakwood desk in a sombre office, emotionless. He would then dish out his decision to date Miss Perfect in the same tone of voice he did to each and every one of his clients.

"Great I will pick you up on Friday night shall we say about half past six?"

"Yeah great see you then!"

"Ok bye then"

And with that he was gone. So I now have two and bit days to preen and pretty myself so that I look totally amazing. He needs to know that I have absolutely flourished without him in my life (even though I haven't and think about him all the time). This will have to be the works! I'm going to be every inch the diva that doesn't have time for insignificant things like men! I'm fired up beyond belief I'm going to do it, so much to think about in such little time.

Thursday 7th July
Preparing for the 'un date'

Perfection isn't going to be easy! Frantic . . . Yes! Totally! Just so you don't mistake my intentions-This is a form of self-defence. He is more or less going to tell me I'm dumped. Never one to be the screeching school girl who runs and hides in the ladies once it's over, only to be traumatised well into adult life. No I am an adult and I am going to act like one! This will involve firstly going to my appointment at the nail bar at 10am to get a full set of ultra-glamorous acrylics put on. The lunch with Sebastian will be at mid-day, he wants to know what I am doing with my leave but also to see the shiny new nails.

At 2pm I am treating myself to a massage at my favourite spa in town, I figured that this would relax everything and give me a glowing aura. This was always good when meeting a soon-to-be-if-not-already-ex-boyfriend! Then on Friday morning day of the date itself I have made myself a well needed appointment with the hairdressers. This will be great and putting my hair in the hands of the professionals will give the spectacular results needed on this occasion. They will be allowed to do anything that will take off ten years from my actual age.

That includes colouring, cutting, pinning up or brushing down-whatever they recommend as they are the experts in this case—Just anything except a Natalie Portman shaven head! I couldn't deal with that at this point in my life even though I applauded these leading ladies for doing so I just wasn't for me (although a feminist trip isn't off the cards after I get totally dumped! Liberation is the word!). Giuseppe is superb at this sort of thing; I will quite happily switch off as he is chattering away and entertain thoughts of how superbly wondrous my new do will look.

Then once this is done one last appointment with fellow fashion enthusiast Frenchie (Also known as Francesca at her office job) a good life long buddy who has studied make up and beauty at college. She has done wonders for me on many an occasion in the past when experimenting on my acne scarred teenage skin. She made me a flawless catwalk beauty (in those hedonistic days with a thinner waist and lithe limbs) I know she is capable of working the very same miracle once again on my Botox worthy skin. She is just the ticket and what I need to look dewy and fresh faced for meeting the soon to be Ex!

I am also planning on not eating anything but Muesli until then, I may have to pinch a few of the land lady's cereal bars for absolute emergencies. But while we do not under any circumstances condone extreme dieting at all it won't hurt for me to lose a few pounds. So after all this I will be a sleeker more relaxed version of me with lovely nails and a little bit more travelled than I was a week ago. It will all go towards a much better look, manicured fingers crossed!

Friday 8th July
The 'un date'

After being prodded, poked and had my hair up in rollers for the best part of this morning I feel fairly good. Giuseppe has done a superb job, I left the hair salon with very big hair and it was fabulous! Talk about making a statement! How can I describe it? It's big and red like Jane Fonda in Barbarella, I absolutely love it. With the amount of hairspray Giuseppe has used there is no way that it will flatten for at least another three weeks!

Speaking of the devil, this morning Giuseppe was his usual self and loved the fact that I had left my hair to grow as long as it was. I explained to him that this was down to not really having the time. There was a look that exchanged between us. We both knew that this was rubbish all of a sudden I get asked out on a sort of date and I'm practically running to the salon! He continued to cut away at the ends of my locks while prying into my personal life as per usual.

"So going out tonight then?"

I paused did this guy have a side-line job as a psychic like the woman in Norway?

"Yes . . . Sort of?"

I could tell that my answer had intrigued him; being a self-confessed 'Gossip queen' I knew that he wouldn't just leave it there.

"So who is the lucky guy then?"

"Oh just someone I used to know"

"Oh so it's not really a proper date, just a catching up session then . . . Coffee or dinner?"

"Erm dinner . . ."

"Well that sounds like a date to me darling!"

I could bear it no longer and if anyone could make me feel better about all this then Giuseppe could! There was something about his reassuring face that made one want to spill the beans instantly.

"I'm being dumped actually"

His face immediately did that sympathetic thing where the corners of his mouth did a downturn making him look like a fish; I had always found this to be strangely comforting.

"But why you are going on a date to be dumped I don't know dearie!"

This was a good question!

"Don't worry my darling; we will make sure he knows what he is missing out on! You will look superb by the time I have finished with you!"

Was this a promise or a threat? Still I would be happy to go along with anything that would make him realise.

We met at the restaurant the same way we always did whenever we had met in the past. This was strange bearing in mind that we were going to part ways forever.

Frenchie did her magic too and I looked fresh faced and ready to deal with whatever was to be.

Dashing about in my cupboards during the early afternoon and I opted for a smart grey skirt suit with a fussy blouse that had too much 'fashion' for an interview. It was one that I had kept for special occasions but hadn't known exactly when this occasion would be. Yes I felt like I could have been one of the Creepie twins but only better with big hair, super high heels and telescopic eyelashes! Did I look overdressed? Yes probably but all the effort would be so worth it if it had the desired effect.

* * *

The always immaculately turned out Neville frowned at me from over the restaurant table. He had been working out and it showed. The rippling muscles bulged more than usual from underneath his shirt. He sat silently with me in the brightly lit Palace restaurant. Neville had obviously picked this restaurant for a reason; I wasn't really a big fan of shrimp even though it was all there seemed to be on the menu. I picked out something on the menu that seemed to have the least amount of seafood in it as was possible in a seafood restaurant.

His attention was somewhere else, the wrinkles in his forehead deepened as he frowned even more, he must have done this a lot for them to be as established as they were. This man needed Botox soon! Someone needed to call the cosmetic procedures police this aging needed to be stopped in its tracks before it went too far! He was serious about whatever it was he wanted to say and I in turn was desperate for him to just spurt it out. I didn't want to know how skinny or how amazing she was, or her name or in fact anything about her.

Just the fact that he's having an affair and its over-I planned in my mind to go on a massive shopping spree at Harvey Nics once this ordeal was over. Splash the cash on a massive fur coat and extortionately expensive pair of heels. Waiting with baited breath, every part of me was tense.

"I'm really glad we are here together talking like this after all this time, so many couple's would have given up and moved on a long time ago"

What could I do apart from smile sweetly back at him, God he was gorgeous! This so wasn't fair!

"And you know how we are great friends and can tell each other practically anything!"

"Yes we are!"

I gushed back while tempted to lean forwards to give him a better view of my cleavage. The push up bra I wore was magic and really worked wonders. Not that I had needed any help in that department having great genes from my mother's side. This little bit of extra padding only served to enhance my natural shape which was great and made me feel super sexy this evening.

He took a deep breath pausing for a second before blurting out:

"I'm going with the company to open the new office in Dubai... I'm going to be out there for a year Ophelia"

Shocked to my very core, I was speechless. So there really was no other woman then? I couldn't help but smile widely a split second later I realised what this meant. He was not only leaving me but he was also leaving the country! Still it was better than an affair by a long shot.

"Oh that's nice for you. That will be great for the Company!"

I tried to look as sober as possible as he looked handsomely over at me from the other end of the table.

" . . . Do you understand what I am saying Ophelia?"

"Yes"

I hadn't got a clue in reality; instead I was still caught up in the fact that he wasn't having an affair.

"This is important to me I need to ask you something!"

Talk about life doing a complete one hundred and eighty degree turn! Mine had gone from being dumped to being proposed to, I wasn't sure I could take any more of this.

"Erm ok . . ."

"I love the way you seem to make even the most difficult of questions seem like a walk in the park Ophelia!"

Then there was the oh so decadent smile that I had fallen in love with over and over again every time we had met. This was good I liked the way things were going and waited with baited breath.

"I want you to come with me . . . To Dubai"

This dropped like a lead balloon, for the first time in a long time I was at a total loss for words.

"I'm not . . ."

"Yes I know you will have to think about it and that fine, take your time but I am tying up a few loose ends at work and will be leaving in a couple of months' time. I will need to know by then"

So that was it? He looked at me like I was another one of those loose ends.

"Yes I will . . ."

This will require more than a lot of consideration!

Monday 11th July
Tim and the Big Bird

Today was my first official day back at work, grey dark and cloudy very much like the mood I was in upon waking and realising the day it was. This wasn't a great feeling, I had so much else to think about now with this new Neville-related conundrum!

But I had decided not to let this interfere with daily life. Normality was what was needed in huge doses! The sight of the dull buildings of my street caused a long and pained sigh, this along with the overwhelming feeling of wanting to be back with my new found hippie friends. I so wanted to be in the star van with the twins, Christophe, Amy and Seraphina. They would still be at the Beard Fest and I envied them immensely!

I wanted to be back in Norway walking around in the grotty flip flops and not doing very much—it all seemed like a distant dream now and one that I had awoken to. A dream that was rudely interrupted by the bright red window frames of my place of work. The teakwood varnish on the wooden framed entrance was peeling no doubt from years of neglect. Upon walking through the entrance I was confronted with a sight that I wasn't prepared for.

"It's so good to see you!"

The familiar large and menacing shadow stood before me. I looked to the side of him at the clock on the wall, according to the normally accurate time piece I still had ten minutes to go before my shift officially started. Tim seemed to have gotten even bigger and scarier while I have been away! " . . . You are looking nice and relaxed . . . Nice holiday was it?"

His eyebrows rose with his voice at the end of the question in a really uninterested way. I nodded hoping that that would be all of the exchange between us and I could scurry along and hide in my locker for ten minutes and emotionally prepare for the day. The shame of our first meeting was still very much apparent in the tone of his voice and also in the fact that I could hardly reply to him. Oh the absolute shame of accusing my

future boss of trying to seduce me was still so unbearable! He continued to stand very still and blocked me from the entrance to my haven the staff room. An extremely awkward moment, I wanted out, so cleverly I put one dainty foot to the side of him and tried to make a swift exit. It didn't work and Tim clocked on instantly, he mirrored me and blocked my small body.
"Wait before you go in I have something to say to you . . ."
Great I step one foot in the door only to be told I have the sack? What was the world coming to? Still as I had come back from my holidays a much stronger person I could take it.
" . . . Yes?"
Heart thundering through my chest, Could this be the day I finally get my marching orders?
I waited with totally baited breath for the worst.
"Well you know how we briefly discussed the book festival and how we must promote it?"
I didn't want to be involved in another festival for at least a decade or so, but it seemed that I didn't have a great deal of choice in the matter. His one hand clenched into a big hairy fist that swung through the air.
" . . . While you were away we discussed it at the meeting and there was a vote—basically we want you to be our mascot this year!"
Did I lose my hearing while I was away or did he just say . . . ?
"Sorry what was that?"
"Ophelia we would like you to be the Big Blue Bird! Everyone voted for you because you are the best person for the job!"
What did he mean by 'everyone'? This was a total conspiracy against me while I had been away.
"Oh that's nice"
I did my best to smile through the sheer terror, there was a lot of anger there too. I was not over joyed to hear that absolutely everyone had decided that I should be the one to do the most hideous job ever. The type of job that whenever it was mentioned silence would descend on the room, each body present would sit still unnaturally while the unlucky victim was announced. It seemed that I hadn't had the chance to get out

of it by volunteering someone else. The short straw had been drawn for me and that was it.

To don the 'Big Bad Bird' (as if was unofficially known as) was practically a death sentence, for one's social life. After wearing it a person lost any respect from her peers no matter what rank she happened to be. The suit wearer would be scorned and laughed at; things would be thrown at her. It was well known far and wide that she who wore the bird would be the butt of jokes for the rest of her career.

In fact she would be practically on trial for witchcraft. The thought hit me in a flash! Maybe the dream of the political rally for the destruction of bunnies was a fore warning of this? A shudder flew up and then down my spine as I felt cold all over.

"Was it something I said?"

It was totally everything he said!

"No it's fine"

"Well it's good to see you back!"

Tim stepped away not waiting for an answer, or reaction to this big surprise—away on his heels he was off dishing out orders. He was a natural at it and had obviously been doing this for years . . . Great to be back? Yeah whatever!

Tuesday 12th July
Fabulous Fashion: Leopard, African and Aztec prints!

I need something to take my mind off the life changing decision I will have to make very shortly—but also the fact that I will be the mascot/class clown for a whole day!

A craze has taken over the country, one that I thought had died way back in the 1980's along with parrot pink lipstick and oversized plastic clip on earrings. No they are all back with a vengeance. Pastel pinks and corals on sweatshirts and tight gold fitted trousers are in! Blunt bobs and power dressing are also very hot!

The Ophelia Strainge Diaries

Are they really serious? As a civilisation we have been there already! It wouldn't make any sense to go back to the shoulder padded pussy bow blouses with bright red lipstick!

But they seem to be everywhere on the high street! From the daintiest little handbags to chunky faux fur coats, the whole thing spoke tacky but it's really the thing to be in.

If not animal spots then the whole world loves prints. Big bold prints with sharp colours and tribal designs from the furthest reaches of the planet, this is really a fashion affair with emerald greens and lemon yellows. Current fashion trends are a fabric version of a Picasso painting or even a Mondrian. It really is all too vibrant for words but one can't help but love the patterns that are now found on harem pants as well as blazers and satchel bags.

But I'm really not sure about the leggings I have just bought from a high street clothing chain. It looked great on the dummy but now as I wear them after having just modelled them in front of the full length mirror in my room I'm not convinced. Perhaps this would have been something one could have gotten away with in Norway or even at the beard and wife carrying festivals but not here in London.

A more realistic image for your mind of what I am talking about is: These are a pair of leggings that are size twelve; I always fit in a size twelve! Yes in some brands this size is perhaps a little more snug than in others, but generally I am a size twelve. Although the pair on the mannequin in the shop window was at least three to four sizes smaller than me, I expected my pair to look exactly the same as on the dummy. Perfect and figure flattering was the effect I was going for. The legging's themselves were a weird sort of pale coral, almost the colour of the Financial Times newspaper.

Not great so far I hear you thinking, yes I agree but sometimes we must attempt to wear items of clothing that we may not always want to in the name of fashion and style. Well to add to the strange shade was a black pattern to it. The floral scribbling was very beautiful and looked fantastic on the mannequin, totally figure flattering and great!

At home and on they really don't look as good as they should do! I do not look slimmer and the muffin top that was so glaringly obvious at the festival had reappeared in its full glory. This is not right and it's going back to the shop first thing tomorrow. Not a happy bunny right now and severely saddened by what I had glimpsed at in the mirror.

That wasn't the real me! Perhaps I was still that svelte seventeen year old who slinked around at school like a wispy twig. 'Hollow legs' was what my mother had called my 'condition', but it was really just down to a super duper metabolism. What did I do to be so blessed? I wasn't sure but it felt great, before long however it was gone and the pounds soon began to pile on with all those burger meal deals at the local fast food joint. I will possibly aim for something loose fitting with a tribal print on them next time!

Thursday 14th July
Sebastian has his own way again!

"You will never in a million years guess what I have gone and done while you have been swanning around Europe with hippies?"

I wouldn't have quite put it like that but never the less I was eager to hear what he had to say. There wasn't really a choice as Sebastian jumped on and mauled me that morning.

"Well while our new hottie boss hasn't been looking I have searched online for tickets to . . . You will never guess!"

His eyes beamed brightly at me, watching my every move, this look only ever spelt one thing and that was trouble with a capital 'T'.

" . . . Go on just take a guess!"

I really wasn't in the mood for this after being given the ultimatum of a lifetime.

"I don't know, that eighties tribute concert that's on the news?"

There was a very well publicised gathering of pop stars for the twentieth anniversary of their first group concert way back when. Hey if it was a chance to get that old tattered tutu out again from a friend's hen do a few years ago then yes I would have been well up for that.

Sebastian knew this and looked worried at my sheer joy caused by this thought.

"Is it that?"

He had read my thoughts as it was all anyone had been talking about for the past week.

"No Ophelia it's not 'that' come on we have better things to do than 'Voguing' for an evening darling!"

The thought of us doing the most supreme of dance moves made me really laugh out loud. Although slightly disappointed I was glad for not having to wear powder blue eye shadow with a black and white chequered costume. There was a way of doing the eighties when it came to fashion, and it wasn't in the way that Amanda did it. Big crimped hair and neon clip on earrings reminded one of childhood days spent at the park on the swings. Don't get me started on those clipped on beauties!

Although I generally thought that they were best left back in the eighties there was something about the oversized monstrosities. Thinking back for the briefest of moments, some of the earrings I had worn were not for the faint of heart. Sebastian would have been able to pull them off with a lot more style than I had; he could take on most style statements.

"Well aren't you going to guess then?"

"Sebastian I really don't know!"

I sighed impatiently, this was getting most annoying!

"Ok ok . . . Well . . ."

He paused for effect which only irritated even more.

"I have tickets for Politics Now! How amazing is that? They were giving them away!"

They were giving them away because nobody wanted them, the overwhelming childlike enthusiasm got in the way of him noticing that. I envied the young man sometimes and wished

I saw the world as he did instead of being so sceptical about everything!

" . . . One ticket for you, one ticket for me and another ticket for someone else!"

"And who would this lucky third person be?"

Said with ultimate sarcasm as I really didn't do politics, only shoes and accessories, everyone knew that! He knew full well that Parliamentary debates just were not my thing, I was bewildered.

"Come on it will be great!"

There was the distinct feeling that perhaps his first and second choice and possibly his third choice of guest to this prestigious event had let him down. He only asked me for the sake of salvaging his reputation; he was asking me out of sheer social desperation.

"You're single now that Neville has dumped you! You can't have much on really?"

His comment was a step too far, the record needed to be set straight immediately!

"Actually he hasn't dumped me! He is going to Dubai for a year on business!"

He changed his tune immediately.

"I'm so sorry Ophelia I didn't realise it was so hard to let him go!"

He had obviously thought I was in total denial about the whole thing.

"I'm not letting him go; he's got work to do out there!"

"You want to make sure that he doesn't find a hot Dubai woman! They are really into their designer labels out there!"

"No he won't"

His eyeballs pin pointed to the side suspiciously; did he know something I didn't?

"Ok I won't say anything about it ever again I promise".

Fuming at him; a coffee was what the situation called for. Sebastian realised that he had touched a very raw nerve and softened.

"He's asked me to go along with him"

This isn't something to spread around at work ok?"

"Oh wow! No of course not! You know me Ophelia, I wouldn't say a word! Are you going then?"
I shrugged being miles away from a decision.
"You so have to go it will be amazing! You might be able to find me a rich sheikh!"
His sense of humour was more than welcome by this point. Thinking it all through had been an absolute nightmare over the past few days.
"If you do want to come along its in two weeks' time at the South Bank centre . . . ."
He paused again before squealing uncontrollably.
"Oh come on it will be great I promise you will so love it!"
As if he hadn't driven me crazy enough! What was I going to wear?
He showed me his usual very cheesy grin totally unawares at how annoying he could be.
"I will think about it!"
"Does that mean you will come? Oh say that you will pleeeeease!"
He practically begged me halfway to the floor. I hated how much of a pushover I was!
Note to Self: Learn to say 'No' every once in a while.

Monday 18th July
Driving Lesson with Mrs Singh

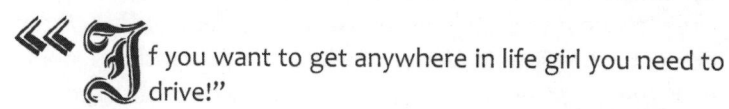

"If you want to get anywhere in life girl you need to drive!"
Mrs Singh declared to me on this morning of my free day. Her arms folded complete with rolling pin tucked away steadfastly in them. Her bottom lip was solid, always a sign that she meant business. I nodded in total agreement but for once not out of fear, I really did agree with her. Driving is always useful in so many walks of life, job interviews for long haul driving jobs is only one example. There were other aspects to finally getting my driver's license, shopping would be so much easier. Being

stylish in town would be a breeze with no need to worry about my beloved heels getting caught in the grooves of the bus floor.
But also the car itself would be a fabulous fashion accessory when affordable. I secretly envied the long legged fashion editors in the city who stepped out of their super glossy cars. I could really see myself zipping around town in a brand spanking new Cerise coloured smart car. Not wanting to blow one's own trumpet too much but I would simply shine in my own fancy car advert! The only think stopping me from living the dream was a small pink plastic card with a photo of me on it (and funding).
On the plus side as you know I do have a provisional drivers licence. This is enough to be able to 'unofficially drive'. So it happened and I slipped into the driver's seat of the maroon Volvo nervously, Mrs Singh squeezed into the passenger's seat next to mine, huffing and puffing as she did so.
"I've been driving for 30 years now—Never once had an accident! Ok so now what do you do first?"
I thought this was a little bit of a practice at driving, something to get me warmed up a little perhaps. But this was not the case and soon realised that the land lady fully intended this to be a real live actual driving lesson.
Instantly putting the fear of God into me I held my breath. I knew what she was like when she was angry and winding her up wasn't a good idea. Ruby had done this a multitude of times as if it was a sport, and she certainly reaped the rewards as well as some quite horrendous results. One time it got so bad that she threatened to have her own daughter adopted. Ruby found this hilarious and from her gleeful expression I don't think she cared very much and would have encouraged her mother to carry out this threat. I simply had to be a good driver or risk Mrs Singh's total wrath!
"Ok so tell me what do you need to do next? You have had enough lessons you should know by now!"
She didn't need to remind me of the disastrous lessons I had with Tony. The instructor who liked to tell me absolutely everything he could about his sexual adventures! Although interesting in a voyeuristic sort of way it hadn't really helped me go anyway to

passing my driving test. But now I was determined and so was my land lady.

"You must check mirrors, and check around the car for small children or animals"

I could tell Mrs Singh was on a complete power trip with this, her voice raised regally at the end of the sentence. I stifled a laugh this really was hilarious; I could see why Ruby found anything her mother said extremely funny.

"Yes! Make sure you remember this!"

Her one finger pointed in the air violently.

" . . . Ok now you put your foot on the clutch and put car into first gear, at same time gently foot on the gas . . ."

The strong emphasis was on the 'gently' part. The pedals however were worryingly stiff I pushed my foot down harder onto it, it jerked forward, after this lo and behold I stalled.

" . . . No no no! You done it wrong!"

This was very obvious, I sighed and brushed my wild hair back behind my ears (this was usually a sign that I was concentrating, developed from a childhood habit and always followed by frustrated huff). I tried again, foot/clutch/foot/gas and it worked. I jerked forwards and jerked forwards again several times to Mrs Singh's shouts and screams. This didn't matter however as the car was moving in the right direction—forwards. Slowly and jerkily pulling out into the street, anything could happen. There were no dual controls on Mrs Singh's car and any mistake could be fatal! Thank goodness the roads were quiet there were no unsuspecting souls walking around for me to frighten back into their homes.

"This is good keep going!"

I was doing it and without Tony, the annoying driving instructor. We jerked a little more and there was that familiar feeling in the pit of my stomach. One I hadn't felt ever since being taken on long road trips with my father at the helm.

"Ok now foot on the clutch again and change to second gear."

What! Second gear! I was happy in first gear why did I have to change this? The panic in Mrs Singh's voice arose frantically as the engine struggled. She was well on her way to having a

coronary fairly soon if I was to stay in first gear. Thinking of the 'gently' part I did as I was ordered and put my foot down on the clutch.
"Yes that's right and now the gears! Change the gears!"
I swerved a little as the change happened, how was I to know which was which they were all jumbled up.
"Look at the road and not the gear stick!"
Ok so staring at the gear stick wasn't the cleverest of ideas but it was the only way to make sense of things. The good news was that we were now in second gear and the engine sounded a little happier.
Thinking that nothing else could possibly distract my supreme driving, it did and the lovely Cole from next door drove past. I instantly recognised his blue and white Campervan. Our eyes met over our steering wheels for the briefest moments, long enough to see the glimmer of a smile. This was the stuff of romance novels! The extremely handsome strong cheekbone structure was almost too beautiful for words. He lifted the fingers off his steering wheel and waved in a shy way, but this was me! He didn't need to be shy any longer. Not after New Year's Day when any barrier that had been between us was obliterated.
"Watch the road!"
By then on our way very quickly to the kerb, it was too quick for my liking. Mrs Singh grabbed the steering wheel and directed us to safety. The swerve became a very rough parking manoeuvre as I broke in time. We both stopped and caught our breath for a second—I knew I was in for it now. I looked to my side at a raging Mrs Singh who shook her head in complete disbelief.
"Just one look at that boy and you forget everything, girls these days!"
I shrugged as there was nothing to say. I was so distracted but glad to see him, to know that he was as gorgeous as ever! He had passed us with a casual wave and that left the two of us breathless. But breathless for two very different reasons, Mrs Singh was terrified and I was most definitely in Love!
"Get up I will drive us back home!"

Saturday 23rd July
Catastrophe strikes

Missy was the best furry friend any girl could want. Even though she sometimes slunk around in the corners looking pretty scary she was still a wonderful cat. She led a simple life so unlike my complicated one, I envied her for it at times. All she had to be concerned about was being fed and making sure she gave herself cat baths every so often so she was preened to 'purrfection', and she always was!

I was awoken this morning by a very noisy cat scratching at my bedroom door, wanting to be let in. It's the weekend and I was desperately hoping to catch up on some shut eye after all those sleepless nights. Nights spent agonisingly weighing up the pros and cons of leaving with Neville. The date is getting closer and a decision is going to have to be made very soon.

Getting out of bed I let her in just to stop the ceaseless noise. She was really meowing at full volume bless her but it was just too much for a tired girl to take. Slowly realisation took over me; the Singh's had gone away for the weekend visiting relatives. I was babysitting her and the cat for the weekend. This wasn't a task that was pushed onto me at the last minute, no I volunteered for the task. Ruby would be out for most of the next two days and so would Missy, a weekend alone with the television and junk food was just what the doctor would have ordered.

Instead I had a small cat with giant saucer eyes gazing back up at me, what was a girl to do. Guessing that perhaps she felt lonely, I picked her up and gave her a cuddle after which she looked at me blankly. This was going to be tricky, not knowing a great deal about cats one could only guess that she wanted something.

Missy then started to rub herself against my legs and purr hard and loudly again. This was a lovely sensation but something within sensed this cat was not at ease. Did she want to be let out? Or stroked? Litter needing a change perhaps? A dreaded task that needed to be done when needed.

The final and most probable thought was that she would need feeding. As if reading my thoughts she meowed in a "By Jove I think she's got it!" kind of a way.

Mrs Singh mumbled something about feeding her twice a day, or was it two packets of cat food a day? The first feeding time being at around six a.m., however this cat looked like it had had more than two meals a day, I was thinking in excess of four plus snacks. Missy most likely charmed all the neighbours with those big mystical cat eyes, anyone would find them hard to resist and put out a plate of food for her.

So she needed food and I scoured through all the cupboards looking for something that resembled cat food. The cupboards were filled with instant noodles and tinned beans or tuna. I had to hand it to the chef when it came to meals she could rustle up a real treat at short notice-I had even more respect for her now. If she could manage to conjure up all those wonderful dishes with instant noodles then imagine what she could do with humus and olives! It was positively mind blowing!

Climbing back up the stairs in panic I shook Ruby awake. Needless to say this wasn't the best thing to do but I needed help and who better to ask.

"What!"

"Where does mum keep the cat food?"

She went back to snoring.

"Well what does it look like? What is it called?"

I needed some clue as to what should be aiming to find. So far there that was cat food-like in appearance.

"It's called Cat Street!"

The girl was obviously not fully aware of what she was saying, could this have been a type of cat food she had dreamt up?

"Are you sure?"

"I dunno! Let me sleep!"

This is precisely what Mrs Singh would refer to as a 'these girls!' situation. Leaving her to her slumber without a proper answer meant that I had to assume the worst: There was no Missy food in the house. This was a bad predicament to be in especially for a hungry cat.

Pulling on my jeans and an old sweater I hot footed it down to the local supermarket. Seeing as it was still very early and hardly anyone around, I made it to the shops in double quick time. It was great having a huge supermarket practically on my doorstep-especially when it came to those late night chocolate cravings.

There was just something about those huge saucer eyes that had broken my heart. While the real folks were away I was her legal guardian and it was up to me to be the best cat mummy as possible. This was a real challenge and I relished in it. After all if one could look after a cat successfully than a real child someday couldn't be that much more difficult surely? This only added to my feminine attractiveness, I could be good parent material one day.

'Cat Street, Cat Street Cat Street' over and over like a crazy person, I willed it to be there-shelves full of them ready for me to load up my trolley with. I loved that cat and it almost brought a tear to my eye thinking of her going without her din dins!

The supermarket was open and deserted as expected; no one else seemed to have a cat food related code red like we did.

The shiny aisles were wide awake waiting for me, now where to start? I had never had to shop for cat food before and 'Cat Street'? I knew cats could be fussy so it must be this brand of yummy yums to keep my little friend happy. I picked up a basket as the security guard eyed me suspiciously; it was his signature look and went with the uniform. Why was I here so early? Did he really want to know? If I was going to shop lift he wouldn't have had any trouble catching me as I was the only one there.

'Cat Street Cat Street Cat Street' . . .

Wracking my brains I tried to recall the tune to a 'Cat Street' advert from the television. Nothing came to mind so I continued to plod on desperately fighting the urge to fill my basket with sugar coated human goodies on the way—but thoughts of those saucer eyes flooded my mind again.

After possibly half an hour to forty five minutes of semi searching and semi looking in the cake aisle I found the pet food. If I was a cat, I really would have fainted in bliss (if that is possible) this place was great. Anything a cat could possible want was here! They ate better than their humans. Every kind of fish delicacy was available; there was even something that resembled Sushi for cats!

This was all really great but would Missy be enthralled with caviar flavoured cat food?

" . . . Focus Ophelia! Focus! OK 'Cat Street, Cat Street' where are you?"

The Cat Food section was in the middle of the aisle, to my surprise there were indeed other customers there. Straight away it was obvious that these two ladies were 'cat' women. Not in the super hero sense of the name but more the type that is associated with anoraks, being single and clutching one end of the last box of . . . 'Cat Street'! Only it wasn't 'Cat Street' it was 'Cats Treat'. It had to be the one that Missy ate. The women looked at their wits end, determined to fight over this box to the end.

In a daze I stepped closer curiously, just what was going on with these two? Would it come to a civil conclusion or would this be 'all-out war'? This was edge-of-your-seat stuff!

"It's mine I got there first"

"So! I picked it up first"

Both red faced and absolutely not going to give up the box.

There were so many brands of cat food to choose from, why did they have to want mine? I inched closer even more to the women who were about to tear each other to shreds over it.

I had to do something to stop this super market apocalypse from happening and fast!

"Hello ladies!"

There was no verbal reply only angered expression's from both of them. They both looked me up and down from underneath the padded anoraks; handbags were at the ready to pummel me with if the need arose.

"I used to get that for my cat but we found something in it, I've never bought it since"

Both the ladies dropped their guard immediately.

"What did you find?"

" . . . Yes! Tell us! What was it?"

Feeling slightly guilty at telling a great big lie, I also knew that it for their own good. They simply had to be pulled apart. In a flash I was inspired by the news story that part of a mouse was found in a loaf of bread and the tail was expected to be in another loaf somewhere in the country I had a total stroke of genius!
"Well I was dishing out some of it to my cat Missy as you do poor thing she was starving"
I had to draw it out a little just to add tension to my story.
" . . . Yes!"
"Tell us!"
They clutched onto their handbags for dear life.
"I found a . . ."
" . . . Go on!"
Taking a deep breath I began
"A . . . Cockroach!"
There was a silence that only ever befell the earth before a storm. The look of sheer horror that was on the faces of the two women was indescribable as they were shocked into total quiet.
" . . . Really?"
"Yes ever since then I have only stuck to the quality stuff, it was on the news and everything! It's been banned in several countries because of it!"
"How come it's not banned here then?"
"Well it's not just me a few people have said that they have seen this happen and pretty soon it will be off all the supermarket shelves, I'm never giving that to my cat again!"
I have never seen a box of cat food hit the floor so fast, the two women decided to look elsewhere for their cat food. Making sure they had left the shop I picked up the lone box of 'Cats Treat' and made my way to the till.
"So what did you say to those two then? I was watching them for ages"
The security guard's expression from rough to a curious one, I could understand why he didn't really want to get involved, it did look like it was about to get messy. The two women almost had their knitting needles out ready for combat.

"Oh nothing much really, they decided that they both wanted to buy their kitties something else!"

I shrugged and left while he eyed me through a narrowed glare. He wasn't convinced as I left the store feeling very guilty. Buying cat food is a very cut throat business and this experience has opened my eyes.

Missy buried her head into the bowl of food the second it was placed in front of her. She looked famished as if she hadn't eaten for a week, it was all too sad. How could the Singh's do that to their beloved cat?

Still it was all worth it even though there would always be a hint of guilt whenever I would recall the incident. I would obviously have to block it all out and never ever repeat my story to anyone outside of this diary. No one must know that I am a master manipulator!

"Where did you go so early?"

The bed head look was teenager cool on Ruby as she played groggily with her bowl of cornflakes.

"I went to get our cat some food seeing as there wasn't any at home! And I got the right one—Cats Treat!"

Ruby looked up at me with that bewildered look she was an expert at.

"But mum made sure we are stocked up on Missy's food! It's in with the coats!"

I could have cried! This was the cupboard underneath the stairs that was a sort of multi-purpose storage for coats and now to my delight cat food!

"What is it doing there?"

I had a look and there were stacks of them. I could now understand why the local supermarket was low on stock. Mrs Singh had bought most of it. They really do love their cat after all! This was heart-warming but infuriating at the same time.

"She always puts it there because it's cool, so the food won't go off plus there's loads of room"

"You could have told me this earlier when I asked you!"

Ruby looked at me wide eyed!

"I did tell you, you obviously were not listening!"

She huffed and continued to play with her cornflakes.

Thursday 28th July
Politics Now!

Sebastian has been brimming over with excitement ever since he had gotten hold of the tickets. He made sure we all knew about it, date time location and everything. He also made sure that everyone knew that they were 'not' going to this event of the year apart from him and me. As expected rumours were rife in the workplace, every time I had walked back into the room after lunch it was to jealous whispers. I guessed what it was all about and I relished the attention that joining the diva club with Sebastian brought me.

There were added benefit's that came with being a part of this prestigious group, like getting off work early today. Sebastian somehow cleared this with Tim using his persuasive ways, don't ask but he was very good at doing this. The Underground train ride was quick and straightforward we missed the insane crowds that always plagued the city during rush hour. Everyone seemed to be going home out into the suburbs while Sebastian and I travelled straight into the city's very heart.

More than eager to know who the third guest was going to be, Sebastian gave nothing away on the train ride. He knew how to keep the suspense that was for sure! Was this to be his new beau? There had been so many in the past year I had lost count. He had kept personal matters very close to his chest. I'm sure that this was a difficult thing for him to do.

Waterloo bridge in the early evening was truly stunning, the view of St Paul's was unparalleled it its beauty. Inspired I could have so written for a 'Visit London' type guide tonight! It really was a spectacular sight. Needing to capture some part of this vision of beauty in front of me I took a photo with my mobile, this would serve as a kind of souvenir of the evening. Granted I would have rather shared it with Neville or even with my secret fantasy hunk Cole the boy next door. Anyone other than Sebastian! Before long I heard the familiar screech practically deafen me once again.

"Come along Ophelia! We don't have all evening it's going to start soon!"

I looked at the time on my phone's screensaver; we had almost an hour before it began! He grabbed me by the hand and pulled me along like a child would his rag doll. He was quickly becoming even more of a total nightmare.

We were instantly confronted by a long queue, why anyone would wait for an evening talking about politics I didn't know, this was by the proving to be totally yawn worthy already!

"I've got a list of questions I want to ask!"

Sebastian patted his jacket pocket; it was obvious that he had spent most of the week thinking up annoying questions. Smiling meekly at him I inwardly questioned myself and what I was doing there in the overly bright lobby. The harsh florescent lighting left absolutely nothing to the imagination, no place to hide my lumps and bumps. No amount of breathing in was going to make me look svelte in the sensible jersey top and smart trousers. Kept for special occasions I hadn't realised how much I had changed since I last wore this outfit.

The crowds buzzed, the great public had begun to pour into the swish looking lobby. I spied a few politician-looking types that were to be expected. My eyes scoured the crowds looking for someone that I recognised, someone who would take the illustrious place of 'third ticket holder', and someone who could share the misery with me. I could see the extreme excitement in Sebastian's body language; the tension radiated off him in powerful waves. Did he think that Joan Collins would be walking through the lobby at any moment? Decked out head to toe in her dazzling jewels, he would have bowed down and been her most subservient follower for the evening. He was a devoted follower. But wait! Perhaps she would be the third person? I waited with baited breath.

"It's a shame that we haven't got a third person!"

"You mean it's just the two of us?"

"Yep afraid so, no one else wanted to come along but I knew you would!"

He looked at me his gaze thoughtful and thanking even though I felt like a total wally. I was obviously the last choice, well that was just great!

"It's a real shame, a waste of a ticket . . ."

Yes it was, but not for long . . .

"Excuse me did you say that you had a spare ticket going?"

The spottiest teenager ever known to humankind emerged from nowhere! Small and gnarled the thing that stood before us resembled a terrible version of a garden gnome just a bit bigger and with the ability to speak.

"It's for my Mum, I thought I could get her in but they are fully booked!"

While I should have taken pity on the kid I couldn't help but stare in a horrified awe at his straw like dry hair. This was no doubt due to an excess of hair products smeared through his barnet, a typical teenage obsession. Slender in build and looking extremely undernourished, he must have been living on a staple diet of crisps and biscuits! He had all the signs of a kid afflicted with the dread disease of 'studentism'. Sebastian was just as appalled as I was and took sharp intake of breath with a quick step back. The whites of his eyes were visible all around his dilated pupils as he thought about it. Here was a chance to make some easy money and Sebastian would never turn that down. Anything that went towards helping him fund his designer habit.

"I will give you my spare ticket for ten pounds"

I was in total shock as the business man in Sebastian came out.

"I thought you got these tickets for fr . . ."

Sebastian shot a look in my direction that told me to shut up instantly. I did what I was told and bit my lips but it was too late the spotty kid had clocked onto what was going on.

"'Free' did you say?"

He looked at me wide eyed, Sebastian interrupted this battle of wills—well my will wasn't very strong so technically it wasn't a battle from my side.

"You can have it for £7 and that's it!"

" . . . Five pounds!"

" . . . Six pounds fifty!"
" . . . Six pounds!"
" . . . Done!"
The kid pulled out the wad of notes and paid up; his proud and extra smiley mother looked on at the exchange. She looked the epitome of maternal in her floral shift dress, pristine white handbag slung over her forearm and matching flat shoes. She could have been a nicer version of my own mother.
"Well that can go towards refreshments later!"
Sebastian winked and pocketed the cold hard cash quickly. The four of us were ushered into the dark auditorium soon after that I was glad of the dark it hid what I felt was the cheap mascara starting to run from the corners of my eyes. I was not however glad of how one of my kitten heels got caught in a small corner of rough carpet that had come loose from the floor. I steadied myself by grabbing the nearest back rest of a chair and narrowly missing a fellow guest by millimetres.
"Hello people! Our seats they are over here!"
Sebastian's voice could have been heard from the other end of the auditorium, but patience was called for as we fumbled our way through the dark to our seats. Directly in front of the stage we would be able to see everything I was impressed with Sebastian, not only did he get free tickets but they were also in a great spot. He really was the boy wonder; however tickets to see something else would have been preferable. I fantasized about that eighties concert that was happening in town sometime this week. Why couldn't we have gone to that and had a great evening singing along to the mighty pop greats? This wasn't in my fate as Mrs Singh would say, so I would have to just bear the rest of the evening seated in between Sebastian and the spotty kid's mother. I smoothed down my dress and flattened down my jersey top, it had begun to ride up my waist-very embarrassing! I also wished I had put on a fresh layer of lipstick before I had entered the darkness. Looking washed out on my TV debut was not an option. I felt sad at the lost opportunity for a career in television.
Before this could be pondered further the lights dimmed, the soft spot lights that had helped us to our seats switched off

completely with only the main light on the stage. This was high drama at its classiest!

The thunderous applause came out of nowhere as the large TV cameras moved into position on the floor surrounding the stage. I blinked and the panel of speakers had arrived and taken their places.

"Welcome to this week's Politics Now! coming from the Southbank Centre, London. Today our guests include . . . ."

To my sheer shock and horror there was spotty kid, he was seated amongst the guests! I knew he didn't have enough tickets but surely someone would have to get rid of him. Unless there was the remotest possibility that he was meant to sit there all superior to us mere mortals! My jaw could not have dropped any faster. He waved briefly to the audience as he was introduced as a representative to the National Union of College Students. Sebastian was just as shocked as I was he mouthed the unmistakable words 'Oh my God' over in my direction. Or at least that's what it looked like he said.

The mother who had spawned spotty kid was extremely proud.

"That's my Boy!"

She couldn't have grinned any more widely than she did. Then the politics began, I was bored within seconds of the first speaker beginning her short announcement. There was one thing that seemed to keep me occupied for a little longer than normal when it came to this sort of thing-The pale green pumps she wore. These were very interesting in a very retro way, (which as we know is making a huge comeback in fashion).

An instantaneous fashion digression was brought on by these green pumps: Shocking as it is to believe yes pumps in all their glory and colours of the rainbow are back with a vengeance! These with shoulder pads and clip on faux pearl earrings are back on boutique window dummies everywhere.

Anything from pastel 'Pretty in Pink' style sweat tops to neon earrings and 'jellies' we love it all. For this summer's fashion think Dirty Dancing's Baby mixed with Flashdance, Fame and a sprinkling of the magical Olivia Newton John. Fashion is fitted feminine and sexy as well as loose and carefree!

Back to Politics Now! And I loved how these green pumps clashed stylishly with the pillar box red jumpsuit she wore with her matching nails. Reminiscent of a track suit it was teamed with a chunky gold neck piece of costume jewellery. She certainly stood out I wished I had the guts to walk around in such a strangely alluring ensemble. One was usually quite hasty to dismiss clothing and accessories that are inspired from the wilder decades; it took a certain level of bravery and time to put together something that looked edgy but acceptable.

Apart from that there was nothing else to hold my interest. I soon began to doze off again, this developed into a shallow 'half' nap that didn't last long, Sebastian nudged me hard in the ribs. This wasn't appreciated at all as one can imagine.

"Libraries are an integral part of life in this country; we will aim to sustain them for as long as we possibly can . . ."

Sebastian raised his hand higher than anyone else could; he had that 'determined' look. He wanted to screech out his questions to the panel members and audience.

As I expected a large fluffy microphone hovered before positioning itself over Sebastian's rapidly growing head. This was fantastic if not a little nerve racking. Being seated next to him I was guaranteed at least half a second on national television. My pout was an involuntary response, pouting like I had never done before while Sebastian prepared for his political début.

Anyone else would have found this a slightly odd experience but not him; no he looked more at home than ever as he cleared his throat and readied himself to speak. My pouting jaw clenched as tightly as it is possible in order to stifle the laughter that threatened to burst forth at any moment. Please Note: This was hysterical laughter as I was nervous for him (and for me) but I needn't have been. He stood up with supreme confidence and in his best voice commanded the attention of the room.

"What do you think of management in libraries, of the cost cutting, the getting rid of staff? Is there a better way of saving money?"

This was slightly cheating as he had actually asked several questions at once. Until then there had been one panellist who had not said anything at all. But she wanted to tackle this question and slid forwards in her seat eagerly. Haggard and tired looking, she had seen better days. Her bitter down turned mouth opened and a snarling voice burst forth. To a child she could have resembled a fire-breathing dragon. Apologies if this sounds a tad on the cruel side but if I was confronted with a similar image in the mirror each morning I would know that it was time for a much needed career change. Sebastian nudged me hard in the ribs again as he sat down and put on his 'serious' face.

"Libraries are not as important as other services are they?"

An uproar from the crowds erupted that vibrated through each and every member of the audience. The crowds were not happy at the thought of this beloved section of public services just thrown aside like that.

The unofficial spokesperson for most of the audience stood up straight, a tubby balding man with an expression of deadly seriousness. He oozed a kind of inner confidence, looking like he knew his stuff when it came to politics.

"Libraries are a fundamental part of our society! We and generations to come need them, if you think libraries are expensive try ignorance!"

A tumultuous cheer was let out from us all and even spotty kid clapped aggressively. That was truly a wonderfully spine chilling moment, the sort that would go down in history.

The sour faced panellist nodded at the response and remained quiet as the cheer died down; she was not popular.

"Well times are changing and we as a government have to work with those changes!"

Again a loud booing rose up from the audience but she didn't seem to care. Politicians really had to have thick rhino skin! The baldy politics superhero stood up in response, he was here to save the day.

"Once they are gone they will not be brought back, we would have lost a cornerstone of society!"

"Yes but that is the way the world is going!"

Anger swept through the crowds, I was dragged along with the emotion. I was so angry that I wanted to march up to the stage and strip her of that awful looking embroidered cardigan and obviously fake pearls and burn them! Burn them until they were but mere cinders on that stage!

Perhaps politics could be interesting? My opinion on it had changed a little, it could be engaging and exciting—whether anything would come from the ceaseless arguing I didn't know but by jingo this was jolly good fun! Even for political airheads such as myself.

* * *

"See I told you! I knew you would enjoy it! I bet you are glad you came now!"

It was a superb evening and even more fantastic was the fact that I was going to be on television! I hoped my pout would show up. Sebastian left me at the station and went off his own way. As soon as he was out of sight I fumbled in my bag for my mobile. There was something important that needed to be done. My heart pounded at the thought as I waited at the cold dark station. There were so many questions that were still unanswered but I remembered a quote from a film that 'a life lived in fear is a life half lived', perhaps my bravado was brought on by the nights activities, the feeling as we had left the studio's was infectious, like a drug I revelled in it. Yes I had there and then made my decision.

The few people that were on the carriage were probably sleeping off a very good evening, the young man who sat opposite me looked like he had a fair few and was practically unable to move or make sense of anything around him despite the angry florescent lighting on the carriage. I looked the time on the phones screen. It was midnight this was very poignant in a Cinderella sort of way.

"Ophelia"

His voice was wispy sounding as if he was about to nod off to sleep

"Neville I'm sorry it's late . . . I want to come with you!"

There was a pause on the other end of the line. Perhaps he needed time to take in the good news?

"That's really great darling! I'm so pleased! I promise I will do everything to make you as happy as possible!"

His answer seemed automated but that was ok. I felt a sense of real relief at the fact that I had made a decision at last. Yes it was going to be a great move how could it not be? This was Dubai the capital city of the financial world at the moment. However no sooner had I made the statement did the cool of the night air chill me to the bone. I really was going to have to say goodbye to everything I knew.

"That's really great Ophelia, but I must go I have to be up for a really important meeting tomorrow morning, first thing you know how it is!"

"Yes sure, goodnight then"

I didn't have a clue how it was, I must have just caught him at a bad moment after a long day. There were more important things to consider now as I made my way home in the grotty underground carriage. Everything would be so much better in Dubai! I began to ponder on things such as: Would the people of Dubai appreciate the beautiful Geisha wedge heels more than the folk of London? I'm sure with the glossy skyscrapers and shiny malls that I have heard so much about they would love my quirky fashion sense. With a sigh of total happiness I finally felt as though thing were going my way.

Monday 1st August
Snail cream

I know! Yes at first we have piranha pedicures and now its cream made from snail excrement of all things! But not just any snails that are found in your back garden, these are specially bred snails whose excrement is known far and wide for its blemish control properties. Perhaps it's something in their diet? Now here's the science bit, snail cream claims to reduce the onset of wrinkles, and helps cells 'rejuvenate'. How fabulous is that? Apparently Chilean snail farmers saw that their wounded rough skin started to heal much quicker when they picked up and played with snails! It left no scars as well! How fabulous, I was jealous of these Chilean snail farmers and their glowing skin!

Now I like to think I have a good-ish diet and work on getting my five fruit and veg a day. But no matter what anyone does time catches up with us all eventually, but that's not to say that one can't try and escape it? Or at least keep it away for as long as possible through being very sneaky. Telling old father time that the batteries have run out on one's beauty watch and they need replacing before ageing is allowed to proceed? Or perhaps just running away from him very fast while throwing tins of baked beans at him as you do, that's bound to slow him down a little. In the meantime however there is this 'snail cream' and they are selling it in tubs over at the station market. Walking home today I saw the mountain of pink tubs on a newish stall. Not that I regularly make a mental note of all the stalls I pass, but there was something that drew me to this particular one. Perhaps it was the pink tubs all neatly stacked up. It wasn't normal to see perfection like that in a market around here so I simply had to go over and see what all the fuss was about. And there was a fuss with the quickly growing crowds gathering at the rickety stall.

The pots contained snail cream; they had come from the orient so I had no chance of reading the directions on the tub. The only thing I could make out was a picture of a very happy looking snail pooping a pink fluffy cloud. This 'cloud' must have been illustrating the contents of the tub I was now holding.

The small lady who was part of the husband and wife duo running the stall nodded enthusiastically at me.

I was convinced and picked up three tubs for the price of two. If this stuff could really perform miracles then I was onto a winner. Once home I managed a quick half an hour online before Ruby got back and would want to use the PC for her 'coursework' (Facebook). Apparently this stuff is made from snail excrement; this is the magic ingredient so I was right about the fluffy cloud that the snail is happily producing on the tub. I also found that these snails were no ordinary creatures they are in fact posh snails. And we all know that posh snails will produce posh snail poo! How could it be any other way right?

Nearly choking on my tea at this, had I been taken for a massive ride by the stall holders in the market today? Was it all a humongous joke at the expense of the buyers of this scam cream? Quite possibly but on the other hand the argument was that this could be the greatest beauty discovery of all time! With that in mind I decided to throw caution to the wind and give it a go.

It looked like normal cream, pale yellow in colour (Yes this had to be real snail poo!) pushing the thoughts of happy snails excreting into plastic tubs out of my mind I smeared the cream onto my face. Soon I resembled a very pale orange, one that didn't like sun tans. It's been an hour now and there is a slight tingling over my face, this could be the nature inspired facelift happening?

Shame on cosmetics companies claiming miracles for years and making us spend hard earned cash on their products! Yet here it was all along in a humble pot of snail waste. Neville will not know what's hit him the next time we meet! Mega yay for snail cream!

Friday 5th August
Cole

"Hello stranger!"
"... Hello!"

I didn't think that Cole ever came to this supermarket to pick up groceries; he always struck me as the sort who had an invisible housekeeper who did all his shopping for him. And that he spent his time sculpting and being an artist-type person. He would go off for days I imagined to some obscure workshop in a trendy part of London. Like Shoreditch or Hackney to work on masterpieces that would sell for considerable amounts of money. What a romantic view of life! How perfect would everything be if only we could all be creative types? There

wouldn't be people to run the important things like councils and clothes shops. However I couldn't help but envy his bohemian lifestyle, at the same time fancying him insanely-I think you will agree that this was a major dilemma to be in!
But he was here in the flesh! And oh what flesh! I spied a quick look in his shopping trolley and at the contents. Were they the same as mine? (Meals for one and cake was my usual diet)
"So you're shopping then?"
Stating the obvious was my forte it seemed, I was pretty good at it and this was something to be proud of in a warped way.
"Yes I am, there is a deal on the cereal, three boxes for the price of two and I eat a lot of it so I figured it would make sense!"
No kidding! There were three boxes of chocolate covered flakes in his trolley. Perhaps that was the secret to his gorgeousness? That chiselled jaw and fashionable stubble! No I must hold back from speaking like that now that I was practically married to Neville. Although he hadn't proposed yet I knew it wouldn't be long once we were out in the seductive sand dunes of Dubai! I reigned myself in, I had to before I majorly crushed on this guy. But his piercing eyes surveyed me from underneath his dark eyebrows making him look very mysterious. The subject needed to change before he was jumped with some serious animal urges.
"Yes I'm just here doing my shopping, you know like normal people, just doing the weekly shop"
God I sounded like a total geek but he was so handsome. He just had this ability to turn my legs into complete jelly. I eyed the swoon-worthy hot body dressed in baggy t-shirt and worn out jeans. This guy really was too cool for school even though he worked in one (a college to be exact).
"You might want to check out the ice cream aisle they have an offer on the Strawberry flavour"
I had enough of Strawberries to last a lifetime. But I liked this guy even more if that was even possible seeing as he was totally drool-worthy! Now he was even encouraging me to eat calorific ice cream! How much better was this wondrous encounter going to get?
"Oh wow I will go and check this out!"

"That's great!"
And then he smiled! Why did he do that? It was so cruel. He lit up the world in a split second. Christophe and Neville had nothing on this guy, he really was something!
"Maybe I will see you around more!"
He wanted to see me again! Yes please! I was walking on air at our short encounter as he walked away. Watching him with a longing, out encounter had been all too brief! He would also be one of the people to be left behind! I plodded along to the ice cream aisle with my practically bare basket.
I wouldn't need to bulk buy ice cream or anything else for that matter, there was no longer any point.
Mega sigh!

Monday 8th August
Being 'the bird'

The first day of the book festival arrived, one that I have been totally dreading since finding out I was to be 'big blue bird the council mascot'. To take on this role involves an incredible amount of sanity for the first day of the festival. Luckily for me I won't have to do this for the whole of the two weeks. We are too short staffed with two other members of staff on holiday (it's a little suspicious) to have even one person pretending to be a bird for the day. Believe me one day was more than enough playing the part so it was fine. Previous 'birds' have had to do it for at least the first week so I have gotten off lightly considering.
At first glance it was the same bird that appeared on the headed notepaper I saw every day. The little blue bird looked cheerful in the corner of everything from envelopes to post it notes. Then after a few moments of staring at it, the monstrosity of it was apparent.
The larger than life papier mache structure was reinforced by steel chicken wire and the smell that hit me when I entered the room! My goodness! Have I stressed the vile stench enough

yet? I think that I have and you may already have a good idea. If not and you fell asleep when I was previously describing it here's a quick recap—think mouldy cheese combined with the body odour of the countless wearers of the suit. This with a smattering of on the turn tuna fish, basically it's not a very pleasant odour.

This morning I was faced with my arch nemesis for the first time in years, just the big blue bird and me alone together in a room. I didn't know what to say to it, 'hello' would have been a start—should we have exchanged the usual pleasantries before I wore it?

"You my girl are insane!"

"What was that Ophelia?"

Tim had been watching the silent exchange between me and the bird.

"Oh nothing it's fine really"

The whole debacle of a thing was bent from years of over use. This big blue bird that sat perched on an old table did not look very cheerful. Its expression was very bitter, the worn lines in its face told of innumerable hardships and years of misery. I felt pity but also hate for this creature.

Well there wasn't any point psychoanalysing the thing, it just needed to be worn!

So it happened and I became the bird! At least it was roomy inside. The downfall was that the inside of the costume made me gag, but I knew this from rumours I had heard. I took a deep breath of the stinking air and did my best to keep my lunch down. Perhaps that cheesy bake microwave ready meal wasn't a good idea.

"Are you ok Ophelia? You are looking a little bit peaky!"

That was the understatement of the century! Lucy not waiting for an answer then shoved the big head over the top of me. I could have passed out with the stench; it was almost too much to bear. I hated her and vowed to get her back one day! It's no secret that Councils up and down the country are currently strapped for cash but a bottle of disinfectant would not have broken the budget!

"And here is our big blue bird!"

Tim announced with all the gusto of a circus ringleader. The crowds of eagerly awaiting library goers watched on in awe of me. I knew the drill, the hand holes allowed me to sign autographs and flap. While this was a small mercy it also meant the whole facade was a bit of a con. I mean whoever saw a bird for a start that looked distinctively human shaped and had fingers that waved? It was all a bit suspicious but I had no choice. However as I donned the suit I promised myself that I would not be squawking at all, no matter how much Tim insisted.

"Mummy, that's not a real bird!"

The very irritating small boy in stripy t-shirt pointed up at me. Looking at his squashed up little face I was sincerely glad to not have any of my own. The mother hushed her child with a single look, something she obviously had to get to a fine art. He however paid no attention and still looked at me suspiciously.

"But mummy birds don't look like that!"

He was getting very irritating and I wanted to flap at him furiously with the little worn out wings that were attached to the costume . . . somewhere.

Once introduced all I had to do for the next seven hours was to mingle and flap about a little while being photographed/filmed. This was done fairly well I thought, Hollywood here I come!

By the end of the day and suffering photograph overload I was grateful that the bright yellow beak hid my bored expression, a headache was not far off.

I hated Tim and Lucy as they sniggered for most of the day. How dare they all do this to me! I would get them back if it was the last thing I did. Dastardly thoughts flashed through my mind, dark ideas of what I could do to make them regret the decision to put me in the suit. Swapping the sugar in the sugar bowl with salt! That would give Lucy's coffee and Tim's tea an interesting twang! Or swapping the 'K' button with the 'O' button on Tim's keyboard would make for a good laugh (and some interesting emails) Ha! These thoughts made me smile deviously. I was sure that I could think of a few more dastardly plans before long. Flapping my wings triumphantly at my genius idea's before another quick signing, yes revenge would be mine at some point soon (I rubbed my hands together gleefully once I got them out of the costume).

Wednesday 10th August
Life as we know it!

As the title of this entry hints at, it's a month to go until I leave everything I know behind for the sunnier climbs of the United Arab Emirates. Yes it will be all sun, sand and adventure; I have fantastically romantic visions of Neville leading my camel with me on it through miles of sand dunes. In the middle of nowhere with only one another to rely on, from here we would totally fall head over heels in love. But this is a fantasy and the reality will be something different. There will no doubt be pristine international superstores on every corner selling the current ranges of all the brand names. There will be shoppers decked out from head to toe in Armani and Gucci; I will of course need to be dressed in the same uniform if I'm going to fit in with all the other desert roses. I will need to research this further (shopping will be the method I will use to carry out this research.

Mrs Singh's will be replaced by the shiny new multi storey apartment in the high rise that will stretch to the sky. Neville had described our new home for the next year as if it was just another multi-million dollar building. I smiled as sweetly as I could at his description, one seriously couldn't complain at what will be the sheer luxury. My mother will be at home praying both day and night that he proposes to me soon and even harder that I have the good sense to accept. He is a great guy, good looking and well to do, what more can a girl ask for? He's absolutely perfect husband material and well don't get me started on how great he would be as a father! He would be Alpha Dad personified!

Anyway putting aside my glorious day dreams I have begun making the necessary preparations for my whirlwind adventures in the Middle East. First things first I had to hand in my notice to Mrs Singh; I did this with a major twinge of bitterness. The mornings spent sitting at the kitchen table watching Mrs Singh dish up breakfast, listening to Ruby screeching down her phone to her friends about some drama or another will be missed. This was the first and most difficult thing that I had to do.

They were family and I have gotten to know my fierce looking land lady fairly well in my time here. She is not as insane as she first comes across, and that she can be quite kind. There wasn't any reason to dread breaking the news to her and I received a huge hug. Never before was the cuddliness of the woman so appreciated. The warmth of her embrace was all encompassing, it was wonderful and I felt truly loved. So much did I love this experience that it made me question my reasons for going! This was my new guilty pleasure, bear hugs from the land lady. If I would ever see her again was unknown so to make the most of it while it lasted was the only real option. I made a mental note of her expression, every line of her face. It was then so clear that yes! I truly loved this woman!

Mrs Singh seemed genuinely distressed; I had thought that she would have been overjoyed that I would finally be out of her hair. She could at last get a new tenant in that wouldn't give her a myriad of reasons as to why the rent is late . . . again!

"That's very nice you should settle down now with someone good!"

I'm sure that I spotted a tear well up in the corner of her eye while encapsulated in her warm bear hug.

She smiled like she could have been at the much anticipated future wedding of her daughter; I was for a moment a source of pride for her. Mothers were all the same no matter from what background, they only ever want the best for their children. While I was having an emotional moment with the land lady Ruby had begun her calculations.

"You can't take all your stuff with you! I can look after some of your things if you like? You know just until you come back to visit . . ."

Those huge brown eyes peered deceptively out from under her blunt fringe; she was as innocent looking as she knew how to be.

"I'm sure I could let you 'look after' a few things"
I replied through narrowed eyes, she responded with a brace covered toothy grin. A deal was struck with the young sales woman in the household. She wasn't having the imitation vintage Chanel logo gilt studs that was for sure, no matter for how long she fluttered her eyelashes at me. It just wasn't going to happen. They would be worn to bed if this is what it took to keep them safe. Borrowing was one thing but these were 'Chanel' (even though I purchased them from a very high end looking market stall in Walthamstow for not very much). This was about style and principles and they were coming with me. Next was handing my resignation letter to Tim. This wasn't something that caused sleepless nights, in fact I relished in the idea for a long time beforehand. How fantastic that no one would ever threaten me with the blue bird costume again. I was at last to be released from the constraints of the nine to five. This was a dream that I had entertained for a very long time, especially as you know early on Monday mornings! It was finally happening for me, freedom beckoned. Once settled I had planned on becoming a freelance writer, writing for fashion websites and online boutiques. Maybe I could even start up my own small business selling fashion to the masses of stunningly beautiful women. The world was my oyster and I was addicted to the sensation of possibly being an international business woman! Strolling into work that morning, I was greeted by the familiar dullness of it all. It wasn't as bad as it normally was, it wouldn't be hard to say goodbye to it.
The past week was spent fantasizing about knocking on the boss's door with resignation letter in hand.
However the actual moment of 'it' wasn't as glorious as I had first imagined.
"It's in here somewhere!"
The large man waited impatiently his brow grew dark as the crowds gathered above us. Florescent lighting of the office flickered menacingly and threatened to explode at any moment. Luckily they didn't and I managed to pull out the crumpled piece of paper that had fallen out of the scruffy envelope. It had been lovingly prepared once I had printed it

off the pc, the folds in the paper were anatomically correct as far as resignation letters went.

The suspense had gotten the better of him and one gruff hand grabbed it from me.

"So that's it then?"

He surveyed the feeble unfurled letter; needing a moment to take it in.

"Are you sure it wasn't the bird suit?"

His normally confident tone was quieter and more subdued. He was unsure of himself this was enough to worry me. My humanitarian side came rushing to the surface I had to stop this man from breaking down completely.

"No it's a decision I made a long time ago"

His eyebrows rose so high and threatened to fly off the surface of his forehead.

"So you didn't think to tell me about this earlier then?"

This was a good point but I hadn't needed to give the man a year's notice of my leaving date! He had more than the required two weeks. I worked out that this left me a week or so to solely concentrate on last minute preparations (shopping).

"So is that the real reason you are leaving, the boyfriend? That's a rubbish excuse! Can't you just stay here and visit him every couple of months for a few hours?"

I stared incredulously at this man. Was he for real, a couple of hours?

"It only take a few hours to fly there, you could spend the day, go for a picnic or whatever people do during the day . . ."

Speechless I listened on . . .

" . . . And then you could fly home ready for work the next day!"

This was beyond hilarious.

"No Tim I'm leaving, that's my letter of my resignation you have in your hand"

The big man looked down; talk about an Academy Awards moment. His wide eyed silence was more than I could take and feeling the need to reassure him again I did.

"Look it's been a while I have discussed this with my boyfriend and we have both decided that this would be the best decision for us"
I lied there was hardly any discussion—He asked me to think about it and I said yes, it was simple.
Tim was quivering in total shock.
"Look I know the suit wasn't washed, I was meant to give it a going over with some soapy water. That would have gotten rid of the smell! I'm so sorry Ophelia please forgive me, don't go!"
Yes it was true the smell was rank and had stayed with me since that day, it would probably stick fast to the lining of my lungs for the rest of my life.
"But it's not as if you two are married or anything!"
There was nothing to say in response to that and I left him with the letter.

* * *

Ten minutes later and I was faced with the intolerable Lucy, in a situation that I simply could not walk away from. I was practically imprisoned with her in the ladies toilets. Anyone who knows the unwritten rules of womanhood will know that the 'ladies' hold no refuge, it's the battleground of all battlegrounds and nothing is sacred there. The colleague that absolutely hates me was there with her numerous reasons and my heart pounded. I washed my hands and surveyed my image briefly in the huge mirror over the sink.
"Tim said he thinks you are going because he made you wear the bird costume, I said it wasn't and that you were probably running off with a rich man. Guess what? I was right!"
She made the lipstick face as she refreshed the rouge red on her lips. It really didn't do much for her complexion; deep red was a shade that only the very brave would take a chance on. Lucy was too covered in fake tan for it to work effectively, and was an image I will never forget. In fact it was therapy inducing! Things had been strained between us over the past year I didn't know why, but they had gotten worse since Tim

arrived. Lucy and her obsessive need to be everywhere he was and wanting to be the only member of staff that he spoke to was overwhelming. This was an aspect to my job that I was not going to miss.

"Yes I have met someone and I'm moving out there for a fresh start!"

I rubbed a quick dose of strawberry lip balm over my parched lips. Lucy was not going to let this battle of wills go just like that.

"Oh right . . ."

She turned to me and away from the large mirror and barked "So what are you running from? I just don't understand what Tim sees in you!"

She stormed out her heels clicking hard on the tiled floor leaving an utterly confused and shocked Ophelia in the loos. Should I have been flattered? Erm . . . . No! Lucy was totally delusional and imagined the whole thing. Whatever the case was I couldn't wait to get away from the gossip. You would be very surprised at what goes on between the bookshelves in a library!

* * *

"Are you absolutely sure about this Ophelia? Is this not just another one of your love affairs?"

Mother and I sat over afternoon tea last week; she managed to slot me in before her afternoon bridge club.

"No I have made this decision after a lot of thought!"

I stated this with every bit of energy I had, did this sound just as delusional as something Lucy would say? Her face watched mine and for the first time in a long time she was concerned.

"I worry about you Ophelia, you know there is always a place for you here, your room is always here for you darling!"

My father completely oblivious to the deep meaningful continued to pour his complete concentration onto the daily papers. He had done this religiously for years, taking in every fact and figure he could on politics, sport, current affairs, you

name it and he was there. Perhaps it was his way of getting away from my mother's overwhelming Oestrogen levels?
Today she was calm and collected which made a difference. With love she grabbed onto my hand and held it on the soft dining table cloth from where she sat opposite me. There was a strange sens of déjà vu as we sat almost in exactly the same position as I had with the strange fortune teller in Norway. But she was more soothing and softer towards me. Drawing back her hand away from mine, I watched her sip the rest of her tea. The wrinkles on her top lip scrunched up the way she always did during periods of deep thought. She was really away with the fairies for a second before coming back to reality.

"Right I'd better be going now I don't have long to get there!" Practically jumping out of her seat she grabbed her handbag and rushed off. She left me with the thought of being back in my pink frilled room once again. A little frightening, I was then the one to be concerned knowing that she must have puffed up the cushions and vacuumed every day since leaving. Yes I should be grateful it's a place to stay and apologies for my lack of gratitude, but with the room will come all the responsibilities. These included: Having to go on organised dates with potential husbands who my mother would carefully select through a strict vetting process. Refusal of this was not an option. There was also the obligatory extra smiling at all her friends at the various social events she would drag me along to. I simply had to make this trip with Neville work or face the dire consequences!

Friday 26th August
Novelty Mug

My horoscope for today reads something like this: 'Today's interplanetary conjunction means that you will feel like things are finally going your way at long last. However later on in the day something casual will happen that will make a decision for you, although it may not be obvious at first. Call my starline now to hear what massive changes the next few months will have in store for you.'

I looked at the picture of the astrologer with his sparkling grin. My day according to him seemed like it would be quite good, so I was pleased and stepped out with an equally sparkling grin on my face.

Another reason I was so ecstatically happy was that today was my last day at work. I had to somehow get through the next eight hours before experiencing absolute and total freedom. The morning commute didn't seem too bad and I didn't mind the screaming children for once. I smiled over in their direction at the loud music blaring from their phones. Their foul language made me chuckle instead of scowl. Yes things couldn't be better, as after today any visiting I would be doing would be done in a chauffeur driven car. This would probably be quite a nice car, big roomy and covered with luscious leather on the inside. I sighed languishing in this luxurious thought it's going to be wonderful.

After a day of smiling at the normally tedious public for one last time, I grabbed my things ready to go home.

" . . . Oh no you're not! We have a surprise for you!"

Lucy did her best to smile and I appreciated the effort. So it happened that the three of us ended up at the local for a 'quick drink'. There was no Sebastian he had called in sick that morning, his voice cracked up as I answered the phone, he did sound awful.

"I'm not well so I'm staying in bed, I'm sorry about not coming out to play tonight!"

The real reason he wasn't coming was that he was sad; he would be the only person that would miss my presence at the library.

So there we were at our local stomping ground, it was a quiet night this was odd seeing as it was a Friday night. There were the usual odd balls hanging around, people with no homes to go to. Or homes that perhaps they didn't want to go back to, ones with nagging spouses?

The three of us took the corner bench, and I felt instantly that I had walked in on a bad date.

Did Tim feel the same way about Lucy as she quite visibly did about him? I didn't have to be a body language expert to decipher Lucy's smiling and giggling at every word that Tim uttered. Even if he would want to talk about haemorrhoids she would love it.

"Tim and I have got you a little something seeing as you are leaving!"

Was it me or was she doing the whole 'Tim and I' routine a lot these days? Perhaps there really was something going on here that I didn't know about? Well as they say 'silence is golden' and I hoped it would shine its rays this evening and get me through it. I had promised myself a hot bubble bath with celebratory glass of wine, this was really where one preferred to be instead of being stuck in the grey work trousers with a waistband that seemed to be getting tighter with every second.

My sober looking blouse clung to me as the pub got warmer; things were positively steaming between my two soon to be ex-colleagues.

Lucy pulled out a crudely wrapped parcel; I was sure the wrapping was Christmas themed but not wanting to rock the boat I smiled and accepted it with as much grace as I could muster.

" . . . For moi? Oh you shouldn't have!"

Un-wrapping the blob shaped gift was not the easiest of tasks. There was so much paper it was unbelievable. I laughed off yet another layer of paper, after a while getting to the lower epidermis of the thing. It was clear to see that it was fairly small and rectangular.

The two egged me on the final leg of my unwrapping race, I was nearly there! And before long I was faced with a box that said 'Novelty Mug' on it. Most people would have been insulted and cried, and I like most people was but I held back the tears. Instead I surveyed the box in more detail and realised that I too was in my own way a novelty mug (especially believing that I would qualify for my version of a gold watch after seven years of hard graft). This was a proverbial kick in the teeth. Vouchers to the theatre, perhaps a collection even would have been preferable to this piece of junk. Was I being ungrateful? Yes I was and I think I had good reason to be! Hiding the fury was one of the hardest things to do ever.

"Go on have a look at it! You will love it, I picked it out especially!"

I laughed inside knowing that she had probably spent all of ten minutes at one of the many pound stores on East Ham high street.

"It's great really! Wow thanks!"

Things got worse as on the mug itself were printed the words 'Best Pair Ever' along with a pair of cartoon breasts. While this was vaguely flattering for all of two seconds—it wasn't that great. This had to be the world's tackiest mug.

"Wow I will cherish it forever!"

(It would be going to the charity shop)

"Great! Lucy it's your turn to get the drinks in!"

She stood to attention at the sound of his voice and smiled.

"Yes silly me for forgetting! Of course it is my turn and I want to do the very best for Ophelia while she is here with us! Because she needs to know that she will be missed!"

The smiled that stretched across her face was so tight it could have burst. I watched her trot off in those extortionately high heels. It was a difficult thing to admit but she looked quite nice in them. Tim thought so too as he watched her just as intently, it was clear that the two of us had different reasons for loving the heels. Once the coast was clear Tim leaned in towards me, his voice deepened.

"Are you sure you want to do this . . . ?"

We had only worked together a short time but long enough for him to bewilder me almost every time we spoke. The man just would not accept the fact that I had actually left.

"Yes Tim I'm sure"

I stretched out the last syllable in a sort of Lloyd Grossman way, which was in my opinion pretty effective.

" . . . I really don't think you should go, I'm not saying that for selfish reasons Ophelia. Something just doesn't sound right about this guy"

Tim had turned very mystical, this was very odd and I shuffled uncomfortably in my seat.

"What? No I mean yes I think"
No one it seemed could do bumbling better than me when necessary. I wished I was a little more on the ball, but after a few drinks who was?
"Not one to interfere but . . ."
Too late he was interfering! I was saved by the arrival of Lucy back with the drinks.
"Oh yours is on the way . . ."
She winked at me.
" . . . So did I miss anything?"
She craned her neck over to Tim waiting impatiently for his reply as my presence was completely swept aside.
"No I was just saying my goodbyes"
"Oh and you needed me to go to the bar in order for you to do that?"
A bar maid came along with my drink; it was big and bright blue with a yellow straw.
'Did she want to kills me off?'
"I just thought you deserved something exotic seeing as you are going all the way to Dubai! And it even matches the big blue bird! Isn't that great?"
It was quite nice with coconut and a hint of what I think (and hoped) was Vodka. This night looked as though it could get very intoxicating indeed, but also very awkward. Lucy shot a look back at Tim. Who knew exactly the effect he had on Lucy and loved it, Tim didn't even bother trying to be modest and smiled widely.
Her attention turned back to me, the woman wanted to kill me on the spot. What I saw in her eyes at that moment was pure hatred. I felt suffocated and to be honest a little bit sick. Needing 'out' quite desperately, there was only one thing that could be done in such situations—Get to the ladies loos as fast as possible (even though I said about the ladies loos being a 'battleground' earlier)
I grabbed my purse and light stripy summer jacket that went everywhere with me. Looking suspicious I left behind the two deep in conversation. Sitting on the cold ceramic lavatory I had my head in my hands. But this was *my* leaving do how could

I just walk out? Quite easily! As if by magic I pushed the door back out into the pub and there were hundreds of people. Appearing from nowhere this was my cue to make a run for it! There was no hesitation in doing so, and I did will all the energy I could muster after my blue drink.

With handbag grabbed firmly in one hand, jacket in another one manoeuvred her body stealthily through the mass in the pub. One last glimpse at the pair and their worried expressions at the growing brawl before Ophelia had left the building!

I wondered how long it would take the two of them to realise I had gone? The refreshingly cool air hit me instantly and it felt wonderful just like freedom did! The experience of what had just happened was totally energising. That was such a diva thing to do! I liked 'spontaneous' and decided to do it a lot more. Floating on air and merely yards away from home was when the second amazing thing of the evening happened.

"Hey!"

Cole waved at me from his front garden next door to Mrs Singh's, his keys jangling in the other hand he had caught me mid-daydream. Or should I say his 'gorgeousness' was what had caught me completely off guard!

Apologies for turning into total 'Romantical Jelly' but the way the moonlight hit his chiselled jaw was more than I could take. Once again like on every occasion we had met previously, I swooned. In this case being intoxicated was helpful, I felt braver than normal and waved casually back.

Like a love struck lemon, I watched him disappear into his house. He left me still standing there speechless in awe. The cool air of the night air had gotten though my jacket and chilled me to the bone; this awoke me from the vision of handsomeness that was Cole. But what a night! One of the best in a long time!

Saturday 3rd August
OMG! One week to go!

A full week to go left of life as we know it, in a weeks' time everything is going to change! I have never been this stressed out in my life before! This is even worse than going to my first prom. The anxiety is building and spontaneous combustion isn't far off! I'm going to be Neville's unofficial other half for the better or worse, it's hard to tell at the moment. It's the first time I have actually thought about the ramifications of what this decision will have on my life. Ok so we are not technically married but I would be introduced as his 'partner' at swanky work affairs. I would have to play the part of the little wifey and tell everyone how amazingly hard he works and so on. Yawning already! But I would do it because it was Neville and I love him. Yes I really see it happening and I have made up my mind that he is 'the one' and that's final. There's no going back on that decision now.

So . . . Dubai fashion! What's it all about? I have been trailing through Dubai fashion websites and found that modesty and style is the way to go. So I have just this very morning gotten rid of most of my wardrobe. A high percentage of these clothes have gone to a waiting Ruby, especially with her 'You owe me' expression that she did so well. She sat on the edge of my bed making a mental note of everything I put on top of both the piles. One pile for the charity shop the other was to take with me.

"You won't need much when you go, you should leave most of it here"

I looked over once again with narrowed eyes at Ruby who was in turn watching me back.

"I will have to take something out there with me kid, I can't have nothing to wear!"

Then it happened for the first time: Her lips turned upwards in a kind of 'trout pout' like her mother did when unimpressed.

"Yes I know but you have a rich boyfriend to look after you"

Ruby longed for a rich man to one day come into her life and sweep her off her feet, I felt sorry for his bank balance when that did happen. Ruby didn't understand the concept of being polite and not raiding a man's bank account. She would spend the whole contents of it on extortionately priced jewels and shoes! A young Elizabeth Taylor in the making I was proud of her!

"Can I have this?"

She pulled out the infamous pink sparkly hot pants. Adrenaline pumped hard and furiously through my body. My first instinct was a resounding 'No!' There was no way she could have the trophy pants!

"I wore the other day and you didn't mind!"

I took 'the other day' to be before I left for Sankthansaften! So that's how they ended up in the laundry basket!

" . . . Well it's not like you are going to wear them is it? You might as well give them to me so someone can make use of them!"

She really was crossing the line.

"Ruby, I would like to spend some time with my clothes before they go to the charity shop so if you don't mind!"

I glanced over at the entrance to me room. She huffed as she got the message straight away; her particular brand of cheekiness was not wanted or needed, not now before I was making some massive life changes. This was proving to be a very difficult time, stressful enough parting with some of the old gems in my wardrobe. Ruby skulked off leaving a satisfied looking Missy curled up in the corner, I would miss her too and her silent companionship. Still there was no point in getting sentimental over her or anything. There are cats in Dubai! I'm sure I will make a few feline friends when I am settled.

The floral blouse that I bought a year ago from an online vintage boutique at the time was 'fashionably quirky and retro' didn't look so anymore. The few times I did step out with the blouse, it itched like crazy leaving me with a rash on my neck. Embarrassingly red it wouldn't go for ages! The vintage blouse had to go in the charity shop bag with the pastel peach peplum eighties style skirt. Perhaps someone wold put some insect repellent to it?

The partially worn soles of the flats that I have worn to extinction are enough to qualify them for the refuse sack, another wear and they are goners!

After some careful consideration, I have decided to donate the famed hot pants to Ruby; it's not something that I will ever be wearing again. They are precious and need to be loved; the good news will be broken to her tomorrow morning. There would only be room for functional things in my life and my luggage from now on.

The anxiety and worry about absolutely everything to do with moving continents will only be remedied by being with Neville. I just need to get out there and get settled and everything will be fine! Yes it's only a matter of time.

Wednesday 7th September
Cold feet!

It's three in the morning and now two days to go until I fly. I have crept downstairs with major nerves mixed with the most intense middle-of-the night craving for chocolate. Nothing new there I hear you cry. I needed my dose desperately and knew of a supply in the furthest darkest reaches of the cupboard to the left of the oven. The whole length of my one arm felt around in the dim light, my hand having to complete an obstacle course to get to the back of the cupboard. There were several tubs, also a few tins of baked beans. Before long I felt what I was looking for, a bumper value pack of own brand milk chocolate. The familiar rustling of foil packed chocolate was music to my ears! No one would notice if I just took a square or two . . . or three? I loved it but soon felt guilty glancing down at the cat who watched me indulge totally in the silky smooth chocolate. I now knew where her cat food was kept and also knew that she had extra special goodies for special occasions. The fish sticks smelt atrocious as I unwrapped one for her, she jumped on it and gnawed furiously on it. We both needed our fix this evening.

Sitting at the kitchen table was always a great place to ponder things and especially alone at night. There was something soothing about being alone at night in my fluffy bathrobe and matching slippers.

My mind raced while everything around me was silent. Dubai! Was this the right thing to do? I still had time to abort mission and walk away. Granted I would be walking away from a disgruntled Neville, with no job and back at home with my parents once again. But was it better to stick with the safe option rather than adventure into the unknown? Neville is a very fanciable male, but let's face it I don't know him very well.

What if moving to Dubai turns out to be the very worst decision I could ever make? What if it's all a downwards spiral from the moment I step onto the plane?

No, this is just what is known as 'cold feet'. After all I wasn't going to stay working in a library for the rest of my life right? Here was the chance to try something different before it was too late.

Of course change is scary, that's natural isn't it? I am head over heels in love with Neville and I want to spend the rest of my life with him! I'm just being silly and imagining things. Two days to go until the rest of my life begins. But where is the desperate excitement? Why am I eating so much chocolate? Where has my 'Get up and go' gone? It's certainly nowhere to be found. Most importantly though: Why is there such a lingering doubt about this whole thing?

Monday 12th September
Leaving Home

I left for the airport early as Neville and I had agreed. Normally this would have been far too early for me to even contemplate getting up. But not in this instance, not sleeping at all was no fun! Nerves wreaked havoc with my digestive system for hours until sleep finally overcome my exhausted body. I managed possibly forty-five minutes of sleep if that. This was more than out of the ordinary as here was a girl who liked her sleep. This morning was one of those deceptive ones with glorious bright sunshine starting to unmask the coolness of night.

I was now on my way to the airport exhausted after the worst night.

After hauling what was left of my worldly possessions into the back of the cab, the journey to Heathrow gave me some well needed time to myself. My mind still whirred and I thought of all the things that made me say 'yes' to Neville. A just waking up London city was passing me by as I thought. My attention turned away for a moment to the cool morning light that had begun to flood over the buildings. The view promised another glorious day. I loved seeing London town being embraced in the golden light; it always gave one a wonderful sense of well-being. I didn't know when I would see the city like this again. Once I boarded the plane the next time I would see the sun would be over the Dubai city scape. But leaving the city threw up a myriad of emotions within, leaving a place that one knew like the back of one's hand was not proving to be as easy as it seemed.

Goodbye Waterloo Bridge, Sayonara Cenotaph, See ya St Pauls. I could even miss the rain—there was something comforting about the grey drizzle that we got for most of the year.

Real second thoughts were by then forcing themselves into my mind, but that was normal right?

I welled up at the absolutely hideous thought of not having anything to keep me in London. Everything was riding on this move to Dubai being a total success. Drying my eyes with the corner of one sleeve, I consoled myself. No everything was going to be fine; I am moving out there with Neville we will be happy. I will accompany him to all his corporate gatherings and be the 'perfect' partner. We will get married and live in a lovely big house in the country, He will spend his time between the UK and abroad on business trips but he will always be home for birthdays and celebrations. I can of course be a lady of leisure and devote my time to making the perfect home and life for our three children. (These would be our two boys and a girl who would have the best of everything, most importantly two loving parents). Visualising this was easy it seemed like a dream, and until it happened it would be just that—a dream. The rational part of my brain kicked in instantly, was I totally stupid? What was it that Seraphina had said to me on the way to Norway about me and 'suit types' not being compatible? I couldn't remember the exact words but it had stuck with me ever since.

Neville was no Christophe or even Cole for that matter but he was ok, great in lots of different ways. He had to be! If he wasn't why was I doing this?

* * *

Neville had been waiting for me at the entrance to the terminal. Anyone else would have wanted to travel in a comfortable chinos with t-shirt but not him. He waited in a suit and tie, very formal looking as if he would step off the plane and straight into a meeting. His handsome but stern features were visible a mile off as the cab pulled in. Hauling my baggage back out of the cab I half made to greet him with a hug, reassurance was really needed as this was my life he was changing, despite the fact that I had made the decision to say 'yes'.

But Neville was busy on the phone as I approached him. The cab driver who was silent for the whole journey decided to kindly help me with my luggage. It was nice to know that the age of chivalry wasn't completely hung drawn and quartered. The burly man looked up at Neville in a way that was extremely disapproving of his behaviour.

"There you go love!"

I paid him and he was off to his next job. In the meantime Neville had finished the important phone call. He instantly reminded me of an ex, that relationship ended particularly badly so much so that every time I saw a man wearing a suit

deep in conversation on a phone it had sent an unpleasant shudder down my spine and this morning was no different.
"Hi Neville"
"Hello! Have you got everything you need?"
He rushed a kiss on both cheeks, with emphasis is on the 'rushed' part. This hadn't done much to help with the reassurance that I so desperately needed. His mobile bleeped again before I had a chance to reply.
"Sorry Ophelia I have to get this!"
He was off again no doubt sorting out the million and one things he needed to get done before he left the country. This was not the Neville that I thought I knew and loved, I pulled the belt around my mac tighter and watched Neville's anguished expression as he shouted.
His eyes seemed to wonder over to a group of 'student types'. Young and pretty with the world as their oyster, I envied them and their enthusiasm. As he continued to shout he watched them and in particular a long haired blonde girl, she was young and had a beautiful face.
It was clear to see what was going on, I could fool myself no longer. At this point I realised what a hideous mistake I had made in thinking that Neville had ever cared about me.
Yet another case of not seeing the wood from the trees I should have taken heed of all the signs! Everyone had said that I would regret this, telling me to turn back. Why hadn't I listened to my gut instinct? They were all right! Seraphina and Tim, the psychic woman in Norway! Everything over the past few months had been centred on that exact moment. The hints screamed out that that Neville just wasn't Mr Right!
I was afraid I was going to lose him. I had so wanted him to be the perfect guy; there wasn't time to cry but still enough to do the right thing. I wasn't actually on the plane yet so technically wasn't going anywhere! This was good news as I looked around me wildly for a miracle. If the psychic was to be believed then the right path would make itself clear to me. For the first time ever I put full faith into all that 'mumbo jumbo'. I was right to because this 'miracle' appeared in the most unlikely form of Cole the boy next door.

"Don't go"
He simply mouthed the words to me; he leant on one side of the large glass entrance. I saw straight away that his eyes were red; I guessed that he hadn't slept a wink the night before either.

He must have already been there before I arrived, huddled up in his large padded anorak and despite being tired and freezing he was still unbelievably good looking. I held my breath as he approached us.

"You don't have to go; I have the van outside come let's go!"
He half mouthed the words and half stated the facts in the middle of the airport lobby.

" . . . Ophelia! Who is this man?"
Neville was flustered, he had finished the call and for the first time that morning his attention was taken away from the girls and focused on me.

"Neville I'm not going to Dubai"
My heart pounded as I stammered to him. Despite feeling pretty pathetic I was determined that he know.

"What?"
My statement did not compute, he could have exploded there and then.

"You can't do this to me Ophelia! I have the tickets all paid for! You are the one that wanted to come with me!"
The man was trying to emotionally blackmail me into thinking that he cared for me; his tone of voice was only proof that he quite clearly didn't. Next came the icing on the cake.

"You know a lot of girls would kill to be in a position like this, I'm the sort of guy that can really open doors for the right person! Come on Ophelia be reasonable!"

Was he reasonable when he decided not to get in touch for months? Was he reasonable only moments ago when he was eyeing up that piece of skirt, who was probably all of eighteen?

Feeling sick to my stomach I didn't have the energy to fight anymore, only to do what was in my heart. To my relief Cole had begun to pick up my luggage and was moving it towards

the exit. He threw one hold all over a broad shoulder and grabbed the trolley case with the other.
"So that's it then? You're just going to go with him!"
Neville angrily looked over the baggy old jeans and faded t-shirt that Cole wore; incredulous that I could possibly chose such a scruffy dresser over him!
" . . . Ophelia think about what you are doing! After everything we have been through together!"
Those were the last words I heard Neville say as I walked away with Cole by my side. To say I was relieved was a total understatement! The both of us it seemed were desperate to get away from the swine. From the time that we left Neville standing there to the time that we were well on our journey home seemed a matter of minutes. Hardly any words needed to be said, I felt for the first time totally at ease. Cole was no longer just that gorgeous guy next door he was now my friend and he had helped me escape what could have been a really bad situation! I owed him my life! Cole fired up his Campervan and we drove out of the airport car park and onto the open motorway. There was no looking back or regrets at all as we both breathed a sigh of relief.

Tuesday 13th September
Living with the Boy next door!

This was the sort of unbelievably romantic thing that only happened in the movies. I felt like the luckiest girl in the world. Cole's extremely handsome face lit up the campervan beautifully as we drove. I had to look away to hide the mega blushing session that I had when he glanced over at me. The silence was at last broken once we had gotten far enough away from the airport and almost home.
"What on earth were you thinking? That guy is a moron!"
He was deadly serious; I had never seen him this on edge before. There was nothing I could answer him with. Cole was right Neville was a complete moron, at that point I could think

of a few other words I would have liked to use but I held myself back.

"You really shouldn't have even gone to the airport! I would have told him where to go!"

He looked tired; although angry his body had relaxed once the danger was over. The relief had also stopped the adrenaline pumping through my veins. There was also the feeling of guilt at getting Cole up and out of bed this early and caused him all this aggravation. The fact that he had been ready and waiting at the airport a long time before me was mind blowing, beyond flattering.

Just then something very recognisable caught my eye, without thinking I leant in and picked this thing up—No joke but it was a Barbara Streisand Record. Love songs from 1981.

"Some crazy hippy friends left it in the van after they borrowed it! Biggest mistake ever to lend out your Camper van to a commune to help them out! You should have seen the state they left it in by the time I got it back!"

"Yeah not a good idea to lend your Campervan out to hippies"

"I had a good clean out, I needed to repaint it cost me a fortune, someone had gone over it with blue and green paint!"

I shook my head in pretend disbelief at this.

Here I was back in the star van; things seemed to have come full circle in a very weird way. It couldn't get better than this!

"But did you see that guy? I can't believe how much he fancies himself! What did you ever see in him?"

Cole was not going to let it go. This was a good question, I couldn't explain what I had seen in Neville—guess it was a case of the 'wrong guy' syndrome again. The usual thing: It's started off great; he was conscientious, kind and spent hours talking on the phone every night. Then he needed 'space', and time away from me to 'get this head straight'. Well he got his wish, and whatever we had had just faded away with time. I wasn't the right girl for him and that was really fine! I didn't want to be anymore!

But I wasn't going to go into all that with Cole.

"Yeah he's not the greatest"

Cole glanced at me and my meek smile for a second; I truly was humbled by him.

"Then why did you almost go to Dubai for the rest of your life?"

I couldn't answer this question at all-he was right I very nearly did walk away from it all, from him!

" . . . Don't you know that you are one cool cookie and that you deserve the best?"

Early morning traffic began to gather along with the early birds making a racket in the trees.

Soon my mind had completely woken up, my mind ticked over with thoughts. I could always get a cab back to the parents and grovel for my old room back. Mrs Singh would have no doubt found someone super quick, they would have been settled in by now having paid their rent in advance.

I pictured my mother's face with that 'I told you so!' expression on it. One that I would loathe going home to, still things didn't seem that bad anymore.

* * *

This was a strange sensation having just driven back onto the street I knew so well after thinking that I would be leaving here forever. But yet here Cole and I were parked up outside his house, odd not to be outside Mrs Singh's door instead. Before I knew it Cole had grabbed the pieces of my wrecked and tattered luggage and taken them into the hallway of his home.

"You're tired Ophelia, you should come in!"

He muttered to the suitcases as he dropped them against the wall, loud enough for me to hear and blush at again. My silence was acknowledgement enough for him. I didn't know a great deal about the mysterious man beckoned me to follow him into the kitchen. Having been here before I had a vague idea of what was where. I certainly remembered waking up on the kitchen table on New Year's morning. I know you may be thinking that it was just another gorgeous face for Ophelia to lust over, like Christophe, or the very nice gym instructor from last year in the supermarket.

But this was Cole! I went through his bins in the middle of the night! (another on in the prequel—too long to recount right now)

Cole had his chance to murder me and hide the body in the cellar. But he chose not to and I took that as a very good sign that things could really blossom between the two of us.

"Fancy a cuppa?"

He half rubbed and half stroked one hand through his short spiky hair as if to brush out the day.

"Yes that would be nice!"

The truth was that a strong cup of tea was really more than welcome. My insides had been dreaming about a mug of steaming hot caffeine ever since we fled Heathrow! I wondered if it was too cheeky to ask for a few extra teaspoons of sugar, the onset of Chocolate withdrawal had begun already. The kettle boiled and I loved how totally house trained this man was! I could really get used to this!

"So have you decided what you want to do?"

He muttered again gently as he poured the hot water.

"I'm so sorry that was a really stupid question! Of course you are not going to know right now!"

He verbally scolded himself. The half opened a packet of custard creams were a sight for sore eyes! Bet they don't have those in Dubai!

This man was growing on me with every second of being in his company. Here was a guy who knew the importance of biscuits and even more importantly he had great timing with them. I plucked one from the packet and relished in the silky sweet goodness. As if the biscuit had given me an ounce of energy I chimed out not knowing what to expect.

"So how did you know about Dubai? How did you know I would be at the airport this morning?"

He smiled as his big dark eyes looked over the edge of the tea cup.

"Your land lady Mrs Singh saw me in the garden one day last month; she told me over the fence and said that I should do something about it before you went and made the biggest mistake of your life!"

Mrs Singh! Of all people! That lady! I instantly planned on having some serious words with that lady mainly to tell her how much I loved her!

We sat at the kitchen table and there was a strange sense of déjà vu like I could have been there a hundred times already, sitting with him like that. It certainly felt like it.

"Ophelia I was just thinking . . . Listen I think you could . . . Well you are welcome to stay here you know just until you get yourself sorted out, there's plenty of room"

With an offer like that I didn't think I would ever want to sort myself out!

Sunday 18th September
First blog on fashion!

It's been a week since I left Neville at the airport. The next day or two after that night were a blur of getting back to normal living here with Cole. There were at first the longing but awkward silences between us at breakfast, but they have gotten easier to cope with over the past few days.

I have turned into quite the little housewife overnight it seems, content with waking up each morning and preparing the breakfast. It's been the same glorious routine for most of the week. He will go off to work at the college as the Head Art Technician there. He dashes off in a casual pair of jeans and an old t-shirt after doing the dishes (total heaven!). The Star Van as I know it is large enough to carry things in that most people wouldn't normally think of. A few days this week he has come home with student's work that he seems to have offered to finish being the Good Samaritan that he is despite it possibly not being allowed. The huge chicken wire and Papier Mache construction is outside in the garden as we speak and is leering through the large kitchen window.

I have been getting on with some of my own work now that I no longer have a 'proper' job.
"Why don't you try doing something that you love?"
Cole said in his usual quiet way over a piece of toast yesterday morning, simple but very true so I decided to give it a go by first listing possible jobs.
Dog Walking, apparently you need a license for that. I wonder if one has to go through doggie walking lessons. I will have to learn some basic dog first aid mouth to mouth resuscitation really would not be a good thing, but if it has to be done.
I have also thought about becoming a professional biscuit taster. The downside to this very good idea is that a lot of weight could potentially be gained. I may turn into a very large human form of a biscuit. To wake up one morning after a hefty week of tasting only to find parts of me crumbling off-bad times!
I pushed this thought out of my mind as quickly as it had moved in. The last and greatest thought was blogging. I had been writing for ages but a lot of my scrawled down notes had been kept as a rough drafts in an old folder. Nothing ever seemed to see the light of day! What's the worst that could happen? I don't get a reply back to that advert in the fashion magazine 'calling all potential fashion bloggers'.
They want a sample article to consider, so I have put something together. One that I hope will clinch the deal and help me get a foot in the fashion journalism door. Perhaps leaving the library was a blessing in disguise? Here was the chance, if successful to really spread my literary wings and fly. I could finally have that dream career that I had fantasized about since forever.
So here is my winning piece:

Vintage make-up blog entry number one

As we all know when the season has changed and fashion goes along with it! The colours and styles that are in all the high street shops for the next few months will reflect the darkening shades of nature. However a new craze seems to be sweeping through the fashion world! Vintage style make up. No it's not as if we all want to suddenly want to look like flawless 1940's housewives but when it comes to make up we are so inspired by these retro styles. The thick eye lined lids of Elizabeth Taylor playing Cleopatra are so on trend right now.

Style: These are the keywords very much on the fashion cards, anything that reminds us of a time when we were happier and more energised. Think neon and pastel coloured eye shadow of the nineteen eighties, and the brighter the better! Candy pinks, mint greens and vivid purples are so reminiscent of our teenage Dirty Dancing days. One can't help but think that this is fashion's way of helping us fight the doom and gloom of recession, through the sugar coated shades of yesteryear that have returned to our wardrobes like old friends.

Eyes: So for seasonal make-up do not be afraid to go all out and try bold and brassy. Big bright eyes smeared with a combination of pastel pinks with the brightest neon blue. For hot eyelash fashion go for falsies! These will instantly add the 'Wow' factor to your peepers.

Skin: Healthy glowing skin never goes out of fashion, to maintain this healthy aura a good skincare regime is recommended. Especially now as the cooler weather will soon be setting in. Lots of moisturising is essential to keep dry flaky skin at bay. Good skin will give you a great base underneath any make-up you wear. A great tip is to use a small drop of Rose Hip oil before bed; this leaves skin soft and touchable!

Lips: Brilliant red pouts are really on trend this season, a dash of hot red adds a much needed and strike of colour to the darker shades worn this winter. Dousing shapely lips of crimson red or even a coral pink is what to do for us girls! We all need a little glamour in our lives and this is one of the many ways to do it!

Friday 23rd September
Mrs Singh

A chocolate craving came over me and I had the sudden urge to gorge on any that I could find, needing it like oxygen!

Taking a look outside it was the usual deceptively 'sunny' outside; the only option was to take a stroll over to the supermarket to 'refuel'. My suspicions were right it was cooler than it looked, but the golden rays of the morning sunshine lit up everything. The thought of not being here was incomprehensible! The bubble gum covered pavements, dogs doing their business by the roadside with very worried owners armed with pooper scoopers.

How could the multi-million dollar sand dunes of Dubai ever have tempted me away from all this?

A moment of madness that could have gone very wrong! Well there was no point worrying about all that as my Mother would say. I was here and that was that. As they say you can take the girl out of East Ham but you can't take the East Ham out of the girl.

On her morning walk Mrs Singh was huffing and puffing in that God awful shell suit she often wore! I really didn't know why she thought it was a good idea, and it was so not the way to wear neon this season at all! But this morning it didn't seem to matter as it was Mrs Singh-my saviour. A wave of warm gratitude washed over me as I realised if it wasn't for her 'having a chat' with Cole, I wouldn't be here.

She had returned from her walk and was making her way to the front gate of what used to be home.

Missy was curled up in a furry ball on the window sill, her usual spot. She gave Mrs Singh something to focus on now that Ruby was getting older and was out with friends all the time.

My old land lady glanced over at me from across the road and smiled with her quick trademark wave before disappearing. Smiling back I knew that I would be seeing her again very soon, she was still only next door. Flicking back like a rubber band my mind quickly focused on the task in hand—chocolate!

Yes it was good to be back even though I had never left, but you know what I mean right?

Printed in Great Britain
by Amazon.co.uk, Ltd.,
Marston Gate.